"After reading a short story, my highest compliment is 'Damn, I wish I'd have written that.' It must have sounded like a curse-fest took place in my house as I read B. J. Hollars's hilarious *Sightings*, a collection of pitch-perfect stories. Fans of Kevin Wilson, Lewis Nordan, George Saunders, and Karen Russell need to add B. J. Hollars to their must-read list."

GEORGE SINGLETON, author of *Stray Decorum*

"In *Sightings*, B. J. Hollars brings us stories of those on the fringe but does so with an open-eyed awe that is missing from much of today's fiction. These aren't weathered, been-there, done-that, tales but fresh, exciting tales of those coming of age."

DAN WICKETT, co-founder of Dzanc Books

"Each of the ten stories in B. J. Hollars's *Sightings* offers a rare combination of humor, insight, and coming-of-age heartbreak. Taken as a whole, the book left me awestruck, dazed, as if I'd just had my own face-to-face with Sasquatch."

CHAD SIMPSON, author of *Tell Everyone I Said Hi*

"In these amazing stories, which are rife with savagely entertaining characters, the most exhilarating sighting of all is Hollars's adept humor and impeccable prose, page after page. Readers indeed come away with the feeling of having had a true encounter with the fantastic. This unique collection, a bildungsroman at the intersection of private journal and urban legend, is not to be missed."

ALISSA NUTTING, author of *Unclean Jobs for Women and Girls*

"How I loved getting lost in the wilds of B. J. Hollars's stories. Steeped in the landscape of the Midwest, the characters in *Sightings* push against their own strangeness and solitude in ways that thrill and astonish. This is a wonderful, richly-imagined debut."

LAURA VAN DEN BERG, author of *What the World Will Look Like When All the Water Leaves Us*

Sightings

break away books

INDIANA UNIVERSITY PRESS

Bloomington & Indianapolis

Sightings

stories

B. J. Hollars

This book is a publication of

INDIANA UNIVERSITY PRESS
601 North Morton Street
Bloomington, Indiana 47404-3797 USA

iupress.indiana.edu

Telephone orders 800-842-6796
Fax orders 812-855-7931

© 2013 by B. J. Hollars

*Manufactured in the
United States of America*

*Cataloging information is available
from the Library of Congress.*

ISBN 978-0-253-00838-1 (pbk.)
ISBN 978-0-253-00846-6 (e-book)

1 2 3 4 5   18 17 16 15 14 13

TO MY WIFE, MEREDITH,
WHOSE CAREFUL EYES HELPED ME
SPOT THESE SIGHTINGS

It was a small town by a small river and a small lake in a small northern part of a Midwest state. There wasn't so much wilderness around you couldn't see the town. But on the other hand there wasn't so much town you couldn't see and feel and touch and smell the wilderness.

RAY BRADBURY, The Halloween Tree

Contents

Acknowledgments

This book would never have been possible without the help of a grand troupe of family, friends, editors, and supporters. I am indebted first and foremost to my co-conspirators in the MFA program at The University of Alabama (you know who you are), and in particular, to Michael Martone, Wendy Rawlings, and Kate Bernheimer, in whose classrooms many of these stories were born.

I am also grateful for the encouragement of a wide array of editors, including Megan Paonessa of *Flying House,* Jill Adams of *The Barcelona Review,* Caitlin McGuire of the *Berkeley Fiction Review,* Christopher Heavener of *Annalemma Magazine,* Mike Czyzniejewski of *Mid-American Review,* Jill Meyers of *American Short Fiction,* Brenda Miller of the *Bellingham Review,* Ryan Ridge of *Faultline,* Jessica Pitchford and Suzanne Jamir of *The Southeast Review,* Dave Housley, Mike Ingram, Joe Killiany, Matt Kirkpatrick, and Aaron Pease of *Barrelhouse,* and also Jamie Vue, for scaring the typos away.

To Brendan Todt – compass, sextant, navigator, and tireless reader of my work.

To my peer reviewers, whose straight talk proved invaluable.

To Linda Oblack and Sarah Jacobi of Indiana University Press.

To my family, old and new, and in particular, my brother, for using his own talents to support mine.

And finally, to my good friend Sasquatch. Thanks for playing Hide-And-Go-Seek.

Sightings

Indian Village

It was the summer of 1975, and we were supposed to be feeling good.

Gerald Ford had just put an end to the war in Vietnam, and even more exciting, through the hail and the sideways rain, our hero, Bobby Unser, had somehow managed to be the first to limp his way past the checkered flag in Indy. Far less impressive was my own recent limping-completion of the seventh grade, an accomplishment whose only reward was leaving me stranded somewhere in the foggy terrain of my crushing adolescence, another casualty in a long line of those already infected.

Through no fault of their own, boys who had once been stars on their little league teams suddenly found themselves stretched and refashioned, stricken with nicknames like "string bean" and "crater face" with no signs of letting up. One morning they woke wholly dispossessed of coordination – their feet suddenly replaced with clown's feet, their legs the legs of giraffes.

Our symptoms were no different than those faced by others our age, leading us to believe that our shared suffering was likely the result of some top-secret government conspiracy (someone had poisoned the water supply!), leaving us susceptible to growing older.

At the end of the school year, several of us began passing around a dog-eared copy of Stephen King's *Carrie*, which we devoured partially for its pornography but mostly for its self-help. We took refuge in Carrie's predicament, basking in her unbridled displays of strength. Even we boys who knew nothing of the mysteries of menstruation reveled in the possibility that we, too – while enduring the curse of our fading youth – might uncover our own secret powers.

We lived in a place called Indian Village, a small neighborhood constructed on the fringes of Fort Wayne, Indiana. Small, ranch style houses butted up alongside one another in an array of lime green and tangerine orange. They were modest homes – screen doors and back porches – with bird-covered mailboxes punctuating the property lines. The only characteristic that distinguished our neighborhood from the next (aside from the street names identified by Indian tribe) was the canvas teepee displayed in the grassy center of the neighborhood. We never really spent time there (much preferring our summer days dedicated to the icy waters of the Pocahontas Pool or the baseball field of Indian Village Elementary), but our neighborhood's theme took on an entirely new meaning when the rental truck screeched to a halt on the corner of Kickapoo Drive.

I didn't know anything about real, live Indians except for what the movies taught me – all that business about feathers and bows and arrows. And thanks, in part, to an R-rated flick I should never have seen, I'd also learned a thing or two about scalping; how for generations, Indians' bone-handled blades had sliced over the still-warm bodies of white men, sawing across hairlines with one hand while pulling flesh tight with the other.

This gruesome image returned to me as soon as the tall, quiet man with the jet-black hair stepped from the rental truck. He threw open the doors and gave two sharp whistles, releasing his tribe into our otherwise near-perfect lives.

✳ ✳ ✳

It was hard to determine how many there actually were. Five or six, most likely. Mother and father and five or six Indian braves. A dog, too, who throughout the summer made it his business to do his business in close proximity to my mother's gardenias. Who knows how old those boys were, though the youngest hardly measured past my waist. However, the older ones (and most of them seemed older) were broad-chested and gaunt-faced, intimidating in their silence.

Several of us gathered at the end of the block, gripping our baseball gloves as we watched them unload boxes.

"Looks like they're sticking around," Ronald Carpenter observed, spitting into the grass.

"Maybe they'll play outfield," added Jim Kelp, who was regularly stuck playing outfield alone.

Despite our gawking, the Indians never bothered glancing up. They'd formed a hapdash assembly line – father handing the box to his oldest son, who handed it to the next, then the next, until eventually it was placed into the open palms of the smallest Indian who huffed it into the house.

"Think they speak English?" one of the guys asked, propelling us into a heated debate over whether or not Indians could. Midway through Ronald's refutation ("Of course not! They didn't even come from England!"), the one girl powerful enough to momentarily stifle our idiocy pedaled back into our lives.

Georgia Ambler, who each afternoon could be found poolside in her blue and white striped bikini, had single-handedly doubled Pocahontas's male membership just by being there. Ever since school let out, we'd fallen into a routine of baseball in the mornings and pool in the afternoons, a schedule that allowed us ample opportunity to show off the scraped knees we'd earned from our heroics on the field. For several sweltering afternoons, we took turns parading past Georgia Ambler's peripheral vision (our farmer's tans in full bloom), waiting patiently for her to acknowledge our existence.

She didn't.

As seventh graders we never dared call out to an eighth-grade girl during school hours, but in the neighborhood, sometimes one of us felt brave enough to bleat out a crack-tinged greeting.

But not the night the Indians moved in.

Ronald, Jim, and the rest of us huddled beneath the long arms of the oak tree at the end of my drive, tilting the remains of our grape soda cans into our mouths while our eyes focused on Georgia pedaling past on her Schwinn.

Her brakes squeaked, but it was a squeak we'd grown accustomed to from summers past, our pants instinctually tightening at the sound of her un-lubed presence.

Upon hearing her siren call for the first time, the Indians glanced up. The oldest brave (we called him Pony due to his ponytail) tracked her path with his eyes as she rode down Cherokee Lane, two tan legs fully extended.

Like the others, I should have treated myself to the gift of Georgia Ambler's backside. But I couldn't – not with that Indian staring.

❋   ❋   ❋

Much to Jim Kelp's disappointment, we soon discovered that the Ross family's invasion into our neighborhood did not translate into an increased number of outfielders.

"What do you mean they don't play baseball?" Ronald asked, pounding his fist into his opened glove. "You mean they don't speak English?"

"They speak English," I said, settling the matter. "They just don't play the game."

Since I lived closest, I'd been nominated to represent us in our plight for a few more outfielders.

"So assuming they do speak English," Ronald said skeptically, "what'd they tell you?"

"That they don't play," I repeated, "and that was pretty much it."

In the days leading up to my first encounter with the natives, I'd taken careful note of their patterns. For the first few days the braves had dedicated quite a bit of time to their front yard, re-arranging their dozen or so lawn ornaments until their mother seemed satisfied with her phalanx of rabbits and squirrels, whose marble eyes followed us wherever we went. My own father called the lawn ornaments "an abomination of man and beast and plaster," but since the neighborhood association hadn't explicitly ruled against them, there was nothing to be done.

Once their yard was in order, I began seeing a whole lot less of those braves. The only time they ventured outside was when the one we called Pony retrieved the morning paper around 7:30 or so. One day after breakfast I hid inside our opened garage until I saw their door swing wide, the long-haired Indian bypassing a miniature deer and reaching for the paper.

Nothing fancy on my part, just a casual jaunt in his general direction. He was probably two or three years older than me, but I introduced myself and asked if he or any of his brothers wanted to meet us over on the field.

I pointed it out to him, though when Pony remained quiet, my cajoling smile slipped from my face. I tried thinking up talking points, but found myself simply repeating the first one.

"Yup, it's right over that hill," I repeated. "That hill right over there. That's where the baseball field is."

Sweat streamed into my eyes like a doubleheader. I was desperate for an exit strategy.

In a voice like water, the Indian whispered, "We don't play."

"Oh. All right then," I said, relieved for an answer. "Well, if you ever do . . . or if you change your mind . . . over that hill there . . . like I said."

I just kept nodding, as if something might change if I kept at it.

The Indian leaned in close, his dark eyes examining me from all angles.

"You look like Huckleberry Hound," he determined.

I nodded, thanked him for his observation, promising myself to leave that particular detail out of the retelling.

But Ronald didn't even buy the portions of the story I did tell – "Who the hell doesn't play baseball?"

Shrugging, he took his place on the mound, said, "Sorry, Jim. How 'bout taking center?"

✻ ✻ ✻

One night, after an afternoon spent leering at Georgia Ambler sprawled on her lawn chair – fingering a *Vogue* while a bottle of sunscreen rested wearily against her thigh – Jim, Ronald, and I retrieved our still sweat-drenched gloves and played a few rounds of Pickle, taking turns getting stuck in the middle and finding our way back to base. We were playing in the grassy area between Comanche and Mohican when the ball slipped loose – a wild throw by Ronald – and as I ran to retrieve it, I realized just how dark it had become, how the streetlights seemed to cast longer shadows this far from the yard.

Still, I glimpsed what appeared to be a baseball skipping across the grass, eventually rolling to a halt against the neighborhood teepee. I hustled after it, slowing only upon hearing voices drifting from within the enclosure. I stopped, trying to make out their words, but they were all lost in whispers and half-laughs.

"Hey, Jerry, what's the hold up?" Ronald cried out. "You tugging one out or what?"

I froze as one of the Ross brothers tore open the teepee's canvassed door, a plume of smoke bursting from the opening, burying me in a cloud. I'd smelled smoke before, but never that kind. A peace pipe, perhaps, or a doobie.

The entire tribe seemed to have wedged in there, though once the smoke cleared and I came back into view – my baseball glove tucked around my left hand like a lobster claw – I saw there weren't as many as I'd imagined. Still, the four who were there burst into laughter, their high-pitched yips crystallizing as their tongues clicked the roofs of their mouths.

"Yiyiyiyiyiyiyiyiyi!" they screeched, leaping from the teepee, arms raised and bodies spinning. "Yiyiyiyiyiyiyiyi!"

My first newfound secret power of the summer: running faster than I dreamed.

❋ ❋ ❋

They broke our treaty that night. It had never been explicit, but after our failed baseball negotiations, my friends and I invoked a strict Indian policy of leaving them to their own goddamned devices. We figured the Ross brothers abided by a similar policy, and our arrangement seemed tolerable until I woke the morning following the "Yiyiyiyiyiyiyiyi!" incident to find toilet paper streaming from the trees outside my home. Dad had woken me with his bellows, demanding that I steady "the goddamned ladder" for him while he climbed "the goddamned trees."

Our house wasn't the only one to get hit – the houses on either side of us were equally papered – and while I kept insisting to Ronald, Jim, and the others that we couldn't necessarily assume the Rosses were to blame, I couldn't think of any other culprits.

"You don't have to be Sherlock freakin' Holmes, Jerry," Ronald grunted, bobbing in the shallows of the Pocahontas Pool. "Think about it. Last night we catch them smoking dope in a teepee, and this morning we wake up and find, lo and behold, that *you've* been 'TPed.' Teepee and TPed, get it? Caught the bastards red-handed if you ask me, but trust me, old Chief Tiny Dick's gonna pay."

"I wouldn't call that catching them red-handed, exactly."

"What more proof do you need?" he asked. "What if you wake up one morning to find my scalp on their doorstep? Would that convince you? Would this scalp, right here," he said, tugging his wet hair, "on their doorstep right there," he continued, pointing, "help you piece this case together?"

Ronald's speech rallied the others, and he assured us that if we did not take immediate retaliatory action then those "damned Injuns" would think they had free reign of the neighborhood.

"They do act kind of entitled," Jim grumbled. "Like just because it's called Indian Village they think they're the freaking chiefs."

Ronald nodded vigorously, offering up various body parts they could kiss or suck.

"There aren't so many of them," someone pointed out. "Not even a full tribe."

"You think I care how many there are?" Ronald asked as several of us bobbed all around him. "Even if there were a million..."

Ronald paused mid-speech as Jim pointed toward the fence.

It was Pony, his mountainous pectorals and biceps rattling against the chain link. We huddled close like a herd of lawn ornament rabbits.

"Oh, Chief Tiny Dick's just trying to intimidate us," Ronald shrugged. "Don't pay any attention."

But we did, we paid a lot of attention.

He kept staring and we kept staring, until eventually, I broke our stand off the only way I knew how – submerging myself, drowning the world away.

✳ ✳ ✳

Things got worse before they got better. For the rest of the summer, each night we skulked past the teepee we'd hear the familiar yips and screams from our Indian neighbors, which put a halt to all further diplomatic efforts. And in the rare instance we mustered the courage to shout back, our action seemed only to embolden them further. Some nights I'd wake to watch the entire tribe tearing through the neighborhood, capsizing trash bins and spilling their insides out. They were thrill-seeking marauders, except for the nights they weren't, the nights they terrified just by loitering on the sidewalks outside our homes.

One June night I woke to tapping. I could hardly hear it at first – I was still lost in slumber land – though a second round of taps confirmed the first. I didn't look over. I stayed in bed with my eyes shut tight because it was easier. I thought: *Maybe my real secret power is my amazing ability to fall back asleep.* It wasn't. I couldn't. The knocking continued – *tink, tink, tink* – and when I finally rose and headed toward my closed curtains, hand extended, I waited for the sound before pulling it wide.

There it was again – *tink, tink, tink* – so I tore open the curtains to spot them, or at least a part of them – four little Indian asses crammed tight against the glass.

"Gah!"

They turned, grinning, and as they hoisted their shorts, Pony pressed his face to the glass and offered a final *tink, tink, tink* with his fingernail.

I watched his mouth as he enunciated each syllable:

Huck-le-ber-ry.

* * *

The next morning, upon returning to the baseball field, we found our bases flung to the trees, third base dangling from a low hanging maple, while home plate was recovered two pine trees over. The field, too, was covered with trash, the remnants of T V dinners and cake mixes and eggs shells scattered along the baselines.

Things had turned personal – they'd desecrated our home – and it was suddenly clear that Ronald had been right about retaliation.

"It's psychological," Ronald said, explaining his plan a few nights later while filling a bag with dog shit just outside the Rosses' perimeter. "They call this guerilla warfare."

Several of us had gathered near the oak tree in preparation for the assault. Jim thought it a good idea to dress up like Indians ourselves ("You know, like how they did for the Boston Tea Party!"), but in the end, he was the only one among us to don the war paint and feathers.

Ronald distributed our explosives – black cats and cherry bombs, mostly – before ordering us to fan out on all sides of the Rosses' residence and wait for the signal (a piss-poor owl hoot, courtesy of Ronald). Clutching our matches, we did just that, spidering across the street in perfect silence, our heads down and running heel to toe, which Jim (the closest thing to an Indian we had) had heard was how the real Indians used to do it during horse raids.

We all reached our drop zones, but after a few minutes of silence, we began wondering if maybe we'd missed the signal. The plan seemed simple enough: Ronald was to light the bag of shit, chuck it against the door, and then let sound the owl screech.

But there had been no screech – nothing even close to a screech – so Jim plucked one of his headdress feathers and pointed it toward the other side of the house, indicating that I should check on Ronald.

I began army crawling along the edge of the house, and in one instance, accidentally peeked inside the living room window to find the Ross family deeply engaged in a game show. Some of the younger brothers sat on the floor (Indian style, no less), while their parents and the older ones littered themselves on the couches. I glanced at the front steps (not a flaming bag of shit in sight) and so, continued crawling until spotting Ronald on the opposite side of the house.

He was in reconnaissance mode, his unblinking eyes pressed tight to the basement window.

"Psst," I hissed, "hey, Ron. You gonna give the signal or what? These black cats are burning holes in my pockets."

He didn't hear me.

"Psst."

This time, his head swiveled just enough to reveal the sunburned bridge of his nose.

"What?" I asked.

He motioned me toward the basement window, and upon peering in, I witnessed something remarkable by the light of the hanging bulb – Pony pressed hard against the orange flowered couch and a topless Georgia Ambler grinding against him. On the floor beside them were the remains of her now bunched blue and white striped bikini, but all we could see was her body thundering against his like some great rebellion, sweat beading from the tops of her breasts and sliding through the canyon that separated.

I thought all sorts of things, but the last thing I thought was the strangest:

Some day she will be old.

Ronald tapped my shoulder, breaking the spell, whispered, "This was never part of our plan."

Moments later, a cherry bomb cracked through the night (also not part of our plan, though Jim's itchy fingers had gotten the best of him), and as the sound echoed past the trash bins and telephone poles and two car garages, it eventually bounced back to Georgia. She pressed herself to Pony's shoulders as that Indian's ink eyes turned toward us.

We ran, tripping over Georgia's bicycle.

We were nothing but shadows by then.

✳   ✳   ✳

The rest of the summer felt like we were down by seven in the bottom of the ninth – we all just wanted it over. Nevertheless, in an attempt to maintain Georgia Ambler's purity for the sake of our friends, Ronald and I kept what we'd seen to ourselves. We were demonstrating yet another secret power we hadn't known we possessed: our ability to carry an impossible weight. It was a burden we lugged alongside us throughout each swing in the on-deck circle, during every glimpsed interaction of our girl. Some days we'd lean against the baseball fence and watch Georgia ride past, and while the others started in on what they wanted to do with her and how, Ronald and I stayed silent. How could we break it to them that everything had already been done, that the world held no more mysteries?

Despite our burden, we continued in our routines: baseball in the morning, pool in the afternoon. It was pleasant enough, though while the others continued peacocking past Georgia's lawn chair every chance they got, Ronald and I stopped bothering. Everything we'd hoped to see we'd already seen secondhand.

June crept into July, July into August, and soon, much to our horror, school supplies began lining the window displays where once a sunscreen pyramid had towered six feet high. Eighth grade was nearly upon us, and yet we didn't feel any more powerful than before. In fact, most of us just felt a whole lot more tired. Whether we were willing to admit it or not, those Indians had taken a toll on us, and while the remainder of our interactions with them had proved mostly innocuous, this was only the result of our having redrawn the boundary lines – never stepping foot near the teepee, while they steered clear of the baseball field. Some afternoons we overlapped at the pool, but they stayed in the deep end and we in the shallows while Georgia Ambler, quite tactfully, ignored all of us equally while sprawled on her lawn chair.

For a few nights that summer, Ronald and I wandered back to that basement window, crawling up to the soft glow of the hanging bulb in the hopes that we might realize that none of it had been real. Just some dream we'd dreamed up. Some wild trick of the light. We never saw Pony and Georgia alone together again, and most nights, when we peered down, all we'd see was old Pony (Chief Tiny Dick) staring at the television while lying shirtless near a box fan. From our vantage point, his skin looked ghostly – a fresh pallor coating his body – while the rest of us just grew darker.

In the rare instance when Pony and Georgia passed each other at the pool, they never looked at one another directly, adding further credence to our dream/"trick of the light" theory. Still, every once in awhile I'd catch Pony glancing up at her from behind a crinkled *Sports Illustrated,* turning pages without reading a word.

While I'd never known love myself, in my fourteen-year-old estimation, Georgia seemed to have left a mark on him. In the days following what we assumed was the abrupt end to their relationship, Ronald pointed out that Pony resembled a young warrior who'd just lost his favorite horse.

"So broken-hearted," Ronald whispered, peering down at Pony from our place outside the basement window. "Horseless with a hell of a long way to walk."

✳ ✳ ✳

If we, like Carrie, *did* possess secret powers, most remained undetected that summer. Sure, I could run like a coward and keep a terrible secret, but neither of these powers would give us our neighborhood back. Where was my invisibility? My super human strength? Some days it was all I could do to keep my eye on the ball and swing.

That final Thursday evening in August a platoon of weathermen bombarded our TV screens, pointing out areas on the map that looked suspiciously like where we lived. Those men used words like "doppler," "humidity" and "perfect storm," drawing even the most inattentive eyes toward the screen. The Emergency Broadcast System seconded the weathermen's warnings, its harsh beeps bleating from the radio, warning us of tornado watches until midnight, reminding us that this was not a test. Ronald was over (we'd been comparing class schedules), when my father peeked his head into my bedroom and told him he might as well stay over, that there was no sense braving a "goddamned whopper like this."

Arrangements were made – sleeping bags unfurled on the living room carpet, grape soda put on ice – while Ronald and I watched the storm from the porch. We watched as a slow wind began tearing through the leaves, and how our front yard oak trees – once the target of an unprovoked mass toilet papering – now faced a far different foe.

One moment there was nothing and then, everything. The thunder came first, followed by the flash. And then the rain began flying in sideways, like Unser's rain, and as the howling picked up and the stars receded, we turned back toward the screen door.

We stopped.

From our place on the porch we spotted movement in the corners of our eyes. There was somebody out there, or several somebodies – it was hard to make out who. Ronald and I squinted until they came into focus, Pony and his tribe scurrying across their yard, collecting what remained of their lawn ornaments. Their mother shouted inaudible directions to them from the doorway, her finger pointing in a hundred different directions as her children scattered, tucking the rabbits and bunnies and deer into their chests like footballs.

They were drenched, Pony's long hair sticking to the left side of his face, and through all the shouting, somehow their dog slipped from between their mother's thick legs and burst across the street to our yard. This only caused Mrs. Ross's shouting to raise a pitch higher, and I was reminded once more of all the shouts and yips I'd endured throughout the summer, all the Indian asses pressed to my bedroom window.

I left the porch and called out to him – "Come here, pal," – and sure enough, after releasing a nice, steaming dump on my mother's gardenias, he trotted over as if to claim his prize.

I grabbed him by the collar and then – faster than a speeding fastball – ran him home as the world fell apart all around us. Thick limbs cracked and collapsed on all sides of me, but I dodged everything, swooping over branch and under water to return that dog to safety. I leapt the trash bin lids that rolled down our street like tumbleweed, sidestepped the water-choked sewers. I was suddenly fearless, even as the sign for Kickapoo Drive rattled in the wind. I arrived at their home, handing the trembling dog over to his rightful owner, felt the leathered hand reaching back.

I heard a single word whispered over the sound of the crashing thunder:

Huckleberry.

I can't say if it was Pony or not – it was just some old, Indian hand – and by the time the hand laced its fingers beneath the dog's collar, I was already soaring back toward my porch. There was no thank you, just a change in grip, the charge safely passed and then silence.

Ronald began shouting to me upon my return, though I could hardly hear him over the wind chimes.

"Jer! What the shit man! What the shit?"

I didn't say anything, just stared at the dog fur stuck to my palm and thought about saving lives.

After another few minutes of peering into the night we watched the neighborhood teepee teeter and crash to the ground, its long poles clattering like a pile of pickup sticks, the canvas deflating.

It was the closest thing to a premonition I ever experienced, and less than a week later, long after the storm subsided, the Indians were gone. Their father had gotten transferred to Indianapolis, and while the rest of us were out trying on school clothes and stocking up on boxes of Kleenex, their tribe worked in reverse – reforming their assembly line and passing boxes from littlest Indian brave to the biggest.

I watched from the safety of the garage, their brown arms tightening beneath the weight, their eyes sullen and twice as tired as ours. Occasionally, I'd catch Pony turning around as if expecting someone, but she never came. Not a single squeak of the brakes. Then, a sharp whistle, and the father locked the front door while the mother ushered the rest of her tribe into the truck.

An engine started. A gearshift thrown into reverse.

Pony peered out the truck window to see my hand raised high, my fingers tight.

It wasn't goodbye – not exactly. It wasn't an apology, either.

Schooners

My sister Sandy always says, "Roger, you've got a mind like a sieve. You've got to make lists."

I've got to make lists.

Today I will tell you about:

1. Felicity Blanket
2. My father's Hitler painting
3. A raccoon

I think this is a good, strong list.

To begin, you may be interested to hear that a pretty sad thing happened two weeks back, though I suppose it's still happening.

Her name is/was Felicity Blanket (which is the first item on my list), and she lived three houses down from Sandy and me.

I won't try to tell you that we were best friends because we weren't. Not really. She is/was six years old, so we didn't really run in the same circles, though I worked the bowling alley during her last birthday party, and I even put the bumpers in her lane. I guess you could call us mutual acquaintances.

I remember that day like it was tomorrow. I can still picture my freckled-red-haired-glasses-wearing acquaintance quite clearly, her arms and legs flung to the air, pins crashing behind her like sports cars on a bumper car track.

When she disappeared, people figured she probably just fell down a well like lost girls always do. Like maybe her shoe got untied and she slipped on a banana peel and ended up trapped in some well. But the thing is, there aren't too many wells in Fort Wayne, Indiana, and the searchers checked all of them. Also, people don't just go around throwing their banana peels all hapdash. It's not like we're in Muncie.

I really can't tell you much about Felicity, though if memory serves, she was an above average bowler, especially when taking age and bumpers into consideration. Probably, she finished most games in the mid-fifties, which is good, I think, since my high score is forty-six and I'm a full ten years older.

Anyway, my mind is a sieve, and this is not on my list of things to tell you.

But like I was saying, Felicity rode a pink scooter, and I know this for a fact because one time she blurred past me as I was walking to work. She screamed, "Hiiiiiyaaaaaa!" so I launched myself into a sticker bush to keep from getting run over, but also because I thought I saw a silver dollar.

After the kidnapping, news reporters began camping out on Felicity Blanket's front lawn, and last Thursday, lo and behold, there was Mrs. Blanket on *The Today Show*. She wore so much make-up that she resembled a woman who obviously wore quite a bit of make-up. Also, she wore a green sweater with an American flag pin pinned to her right side. As soon as I saw it, I crushed my hand to my heart in the style of a patriot. Then I realized it was just some stupid pin, so I stopped reciting the Pledge of Allegiance halfway through.

"I just want whoever did this to know that we will catch you," Mrs. Blanket told the camera. "That we will catch you and that my baby never deserved this, and if other parents out there can just tell their own children that they love them, tell them this very minute, then maybe you won't ever end up on national television . . ."

Holy cow! National television!

Long story shorter, I leapt out the door, hurdling two doghouses and a fence, and sprinted to Felicity Blanket's front lawn so I could get on national television and maybe even land my big break in the movie industry.

It was such a funny feeling, watching my neighborhood on TV like that. Or maybe, it was less funny than sad. I don't know. I'm no comedian, but I do know that emotions can be complicated, like a Rubik's Cube or a pinsetter or the Foxtrot.

None of these things are on my list of things to tell you.

As I ran I cried out, "I'm coming!" catapulting through the snowdrifts in the style of a sure-footed mountain goat. I only fell once (that mailbox came out of nowhere!), but by the time I arrived all the cameramen were already lugging their cameras by their sides. I tapped one of the camera lenses, shouting, "Testing? Is this thing on?" until one of the flannel-shirt-wearing men told me to knock it off with the tapping.

"Or what?" I asked, smugly snapping my fingers.

He said a word that I will not repeat here, followed by "you up."

Needless to say, I knocked it off with the tapping.

Mrs. Blanket must've seen me, because she gave me this really funny look, like maybe she was trying to say hello or something else entirely.

I waved to her even though we'd never formally met. I was grinning like an antelope, but then I started thinking about other people's feelings like Sandy always says, so I started frowning like an aardvark, instead. I blew her a gentle kiss – almost – though what she probably needed was a bear hug (minus the claws).

Then, as Mrs. Blanket retreated inside her house, I walked up to a beautiful woman in a pantsuit and grabbed her microphone and stuck it into my face, pretending it was a metal ice-cream cone.

"Could you repeat the question?" I asked, taking a lick.

The woman reached to retrieve the microphone, which is a poor reporting technique if you want to get the full story.

"Yes, of course I knew Felicity Blanket," I said, dancing away from her (in the style of the Foxtrot). "We were mutual acquaintances."

The camera was rolling. I could feel it in my cheeks.

"Sir, if we could just have the . . ."

"In fact, I remember her like she was yesterday."

"Sir, please . . . the microphone . . ."

"Well, first off," I began, boxing her out and smiling at the camera, "you have to understand that she was an above average bowler and . . . and her scooter was . . . her scooter was pink in coloration."

The woman looked helplessly to her cameraman, but he was too busy blowing smoke rings to make good on his promise of fucking me up.

"And if you want to know her exact bowling score, I regret to inform you that I cannot release that information at this time. That's confidential, and we have to respect her privacy, I think." I nodded solemnly, adding, "Though I can report that she wore a size five bowling shoe. In fact, I can report that she wore *two* size five bowling shoes. Simultaneously. Thank you."

A few people started snapping photos, so I shielded my eyeballs with my eyelids. Still, my eyeballs sizzled and my head rang, like maybe I'd gotten locusts lodged in my ear ducts or birth canal or something. My mind said: Move your rear, Roger, before these people blind you! so that's exactly what I did. I moved it. Side to side (in the style of the Macarena).

Then, I began feeling awful dizzy.

Maybe dizzy isn't the right word for what I felt. I guess it was more like the inner lining of my stomach had thickened into some kind of rubbery material, like a worn tire or a yellow rain slicker or a...

"This ... this interview is over," I cried.

More flashes.

More sizzling eyeballs.

Locusts, everywhere, and none of them were respecting my privacy.

I leapt the fence and the doghouses and returned home, and it is not important to the story whether or not I cried over stupid, old Felicity Blanket.

Home is a funny thing, and while some say it's where the heart is, for me, it's just where we keep our Hitler painting. Which brings me to the next point on my list, my father's Hitler painting and why it is a good example of modern art. Now, when I say "my father's Hitler painting" what I mean is, the painting that Hitler painted – not a portrait of Hitler himself. Also, when I say "my father" I mean "my dead father" (heart cancer) which really isn't important to the story except that he got the painting from *his* dead father (also heart cancer), whose name was Nathaniel Silverstein, one of the heroes of World War II. Rumor had it old Nathaniel liberated some kind of summer camp, and then he found the painting and hid it under his coat, calling it a "plunder of war."

Hitler was an artist, which is something a lot of people don't know, including Felicity Blanket, most likely. In fact, according to the Encyclopedia Britannica, his paintings can be found in reputable museums throughout Europe. Also, one of them can be found hanging above our microwave in the kitchen, alongside a painting I once did of a schooner.

This fact is not mentioned anywhere in the Encyclopedia Britannica.

Hitler's painting has a schooner, too, only his schooner floats in the Rhine River while my schooner bobs in a swimming pool beside a teepee next to an upside-down monkey. I guess you could say me and Hitler are just a couple of schooner-painting fools.

In case you're wondering, the trick to painting a schooner is to work on the concave shape of the schooner's hull. Also, maybe what I mean is the convex shape. But the good news is you don't have to know the name of the shape in order to paint it. All you need are some brushes and some paint and a good, steady hand.

And I'll tell you something else – Hitler's painting is worth a lot of money (more than mine, even!), which is funny since Hitler's isn't very good. Now, I'm no art critic, but in my expert opinion the brushstrokes look pretty thick, especially for watercolors. Whenever I paint with watercolors (every third Tuesday), I always try to brush the paint on as lightly as possible to avoid making the same mistakes as Hitler. But what do I know about mistakes? I'm no lawyer. And besides, everybody knows that pressing harder on the brush doesn't necessarily make for a better painting. In fact, it can sometimes make for a worse one. A good rule of thumb is to pretend that your paintbrush is as delicate as a dove feather. Sometimes I feel sad that nobody ever bothered to tell that to Hitler.

If you're interested in painting schooners, consider taking some art classes at your local community college. Or if you want, you could try painting a raccoon, instead. Because I guess what I want to talk about mainly are raccoons (the third item on my list), though the Encyclopedia Britannica makes no mention as to whether or not Hitler ever tried to paint one himself. But the strange thing about raccoons is, last Thursday, on the night all the reporters began camping out on Felicity Blanket's front lawn, I was out on the porch thinking about raccoons, and all of the sudden, out of nowhere, here comes this raccoon gallivanting just a few feet away from me. Lo and behold! The thing was about the size of a normal raccoon – yea high – and he really wasn't doing anything out of the ordinary except for gallivanting, which I guess I already mentioned. He had these tiny, annoying-looking claws and sort of stood on his hind legs staring at me, batting at the air – really teaching it a lesson. Then, he pushed himself right into our aluminum trash bin like some kind of rhinoceros or battering ram or rhinoceros with a battering ram attached to his back. Then, he just helped himself to half a hotdog bun. And here's the crazy part: it appeared to be the very same hot dog bun that I had been eating just two days before!

"Oh, don't think I can't recognize you behind that mask!" I told him, but it was like he couldn't understand a word I was saying. Or if he did understand, he was holding his tongue, probably because his mouth was overflowing with hotdog bun.

The funny thing about raccoons, and maybe life, generally, is that sometimes when I think about something hard enough, then that thing will just happen. Or appear. For instance, as I explained, I was thinking about raccoons and then one just came out of nowhere, gallivanting.

Here's another example:

Once, I wanted an ice-cream cone, and then an ice-cream truck pulled magically to the curb.

These sorts of things happen to me all the time, but I'm not sure if I'm the only one who can do it, or if everyone possesses this skill. Sometimes I even wonder if I'm strong enough to harness such power.

My mind started thinking:

Roger, if all you have to do is think really hard to get something to happen, then maybe you should think really hard about Felicity Blanket coming home.

Holy cow! My mind had come up with a pretty good idea for a change, so that's exactly what I did. I started thinking really hard about Felicity Blanket until my head felt like it was either going to explode or implode or do nothing.

Sometimes I wonder what Sandy would say if she knew about my power.

Probably, she'd say, "Roger, whatever you do, don't go using your powers for evil!"

She brings up a good point, and I bet Hitler wishes his older sister had given him the same advice. That she had said, "Adolf, darling, don't go using your watercolor powers for evil!"

But what do I know? I don't even speak German.

All I know is, I'm not trying to will Felicity Blanket back because I'm in love with her, if that's what you're thinking. It's not like we're friends with benefits, either, which would be weird because we don't even run in the same circles.

Most likely, I'm just some normal guy with a mind like a sieve and a super special power. But let's keep that power a secret. The trick to harnessing a secret power is to keep quiet about it, otherwise everyone will want you dead or showing it off.

Sandy would probably say, "Way to keep that secret, Roger! You've got a mind like a sieve but a mouth like a vise," which is funny to think about because if my mind were an *actual* sieve, then my brain would probably just run out my nose like some glorious booger.

That's probably why I'm so good at keeping my secret – I loathe boogers just like all normal guys.

But I love schooners, have I told you?

I guess that's about the one thing ol' Hitler and me have in common, artistically speaking. Though, if you look closely enough at our schooners, perhaps you'll find something else.

Go ahead, grab your magnifying glass, I'll wait.

. . .

See? Right there.

. . .

Look closer. It's as clear as the Rhine River:

We're both one oar short of a set.

Sightings

It's difficult, even now, to distinguish senior prom from the one that came before. Both years held the same mysteries: we boys staring helplessly at our cufflinks and suspenders, trying desperately to crack their secret codes. Meanwhile, the girls had their own mysteries to unravel: hair, make-up, push-up bras, time logged in the tanning beds.

Despite all their similarities, there was at least one detail that distinguished one year from the next. Senior year, Becca Marsden – whose scent alone could cause boys' pants to swell – chose not to attend with her recent ex, Ed Gorman (their falling out the result of a mishandled groping session). Instead, she accompanied the new student who'd lumbered into our lives a few months prior at the start of the basketball season.

His name was Sasquatch, and he was furry, wore 26EEE-sized shoes. Measuring in at 7'9", he'd immediately caught the eye of our basketball coach, who'd spotted him trampling through the woods behind the school Dumpster, licking grease from a yellow Big Mac wrapper. After hours of Coach's coaxing – "Look, Kid, you're about the only thing holding us back from a state title," – Sasquatch eventually submitted, enrolling as a member of the senior class at Wallerton High just a few days after his recruitment.

He didn't have any family, so the boosters set him up the best they could, offering him an engineless Winnebago left to rust deep in the heart of an unknown wilderness. Tinted windows, a screened door – it was all that he required. Though, in truth, he also required privacy, and after a flurry of overzealous crypto-zoologists began making the "unknown wilderness" a bit more known, Sasquatch was rumored to have yoked himself with a few sturdy chains and dragged his home to a more remote location.

Equally troublesome was Sasquatch's brusque entrance into the competitive world of high school sports, particularly for the coaches of the teams in our division. They cited Sasquatch's ineligibility on a variety of fronts, and when our coach fired back ("Let the kid play for Christ sake!"), he was told to provide "the kid's" birth certificate, a DNA sample, a genus, and a species. Coach spent much of the next week working out the details of Sasquatch's genus and species, sitting him down in the library while he leafed through the *Field Guide to North American Mammals*. Coach had only made it through the D's (deer mouse, draft horse, dwarf rabbit) when local lawyer and sports activist Denny Hardaway rushed to the team's defense, warning the Indiana High School Athletic Committee of the discrimination suit they'd have on their hands if they remained hell-bent on violating Sasquatch's civil rights. Fearing legal retribution, the IHSAC allowed his entrance onto the basketball court, despite repeated warning of "the dangerous precedent" they were setting.

Yet three games into the season, the only "dangerous precedent" Sasquatch seemed to have set was packing the stands well beyond the fire marshal's liking. He'd become a sensation, making repeat appearances on the highlight reels on the 10:00 news, as well as earning the coveted cover spot of *Prep Sports Weekly*, silhouetted with a deflated basketball in his mouth beneath the headline: *This One's Fur Real.*

While most of the team never really got to know him outside of practice, we all agreed he seemed like a stand-up guy: never a harsh word, never cocky. When Coach cried, "Wind sprints, ladies!" Sasquatch bounded down the court in six or seven strides, occasionally slowing so as not to make the rest of us look bad. Though three years as a dedicated benchwarmer had earned me a starting spot, I hardly minded losing it to him.

Sometimes, during the away games, I'd share a seat with him on the bus ride home, slipping ice cubes from my water bottle onto his rough and splintered tongue. Some of the other guys complained that he stunk – imagine a dead muskrat wrapped in a diaper – though after a few minutes the odor typically dissipated, or at least gave way to our own less-than-flattering scents. Sasquatch would sit silently for the entirety of the ride, just stinking and chewing ice – our combined fourteen feet folded magically into the seat. All around us, the guys blathered on and on about how much beer they were going to drink or how hard they were going to bang their girlfriends if they let them.

"Like . . . so hard," boasted point guard Dave Malton, slapping his palms together. "And I'm gonna drink a whole lot of beer, too."

Sasquatch never partook in any of those conversations. Instead, he just turned to me, mouth wide, until I slipped him a few more cubes. All he cared about was fulfilling his sacred duty: scoring thirty plus points per game, retrieving every rebound. In the beginning, it was all we cared about, too.

After the bus dropped us off in the school parking lot, we'd congregate beside the cars, saluting the Wallerton Wildcat statue as tradition dictated. Meanwhile, somewhere mid-salute,

Sasquatch would always take his leave, wandering back into his woods undetected. He'd never wave goodbye or tell us we'd played a good game – no ass pats or shoulder squeezes from our center. Instead, he'd just vanish, no sign of him except for the gently trembling trees and a final whiff of his stench.

Throughout spring semester, I sat one row behind him in precalc, and while he never spoke, I'd watched him properly execute the quadratic formula on several occasions. He wasn't the smartest student in the class, but Mr. Hernhold seemed thoroughly impressed by his work ethic and dedication, informing Coach that if the rest of his players worked half as hard on the court as Sasquatch did in the classroom, there was no doubt in his mind we'd be headed to state.

But Hernhold's prediction proved wrong.

Throughout the year, our math teacher had warned us about placing too much faith in probability, and our team became living proof. Most likely, old Hernhold could've even taught us the mathematical formula that predicted our own demise, though he spared us the more complex equations. As far as we could tell (at least according to the stats we saw), no matter how many times we recalculated, the blame of our loss always fell squarely on Sasquatch.

Throughout the first half of our sectional final against Meadowbrook, Sasquatch served our team mightily, running up the score while crashing the backboards, growling when calls didn't go our way. Then the momentum shifted at the start of the second half. In the third minute Sasquatch slipped on a bit of loose fur, pulling a hamstring, and as we watched him limp from the court, we realized our sectional title was slipping away with him. Returning to the bench, ice packs appeared out of nowhere, though rather than place them on his tendon, Sasquatch preferred ripping them open and munching the ice inside. Nobody told him not to. We had bigger problems.

Coach had no choice but to replace him with me – a raw deal – but there weren't a lot of options. My skeletal 6'1" frame simply didn't warrant the same heart-pounding terror as a furry creature towering two feet taller, though I couldn't blame my lackluster performance entirely on the height differential. The truth was, I missed a couple of rebounds too, ended up going two for six from the line. Tripped over my feet, made poor passes, forgot all the plays we'd spent so long perfecting. I grew tired, sloppy, got called for charging on three consecutive possessions. Where was the pick when we needed it? The point guard? Everybody seemed to be in the wrong spot at the wrong time – including the ball, which somehow managed to ricochet off my shin and into the stands.

It was a massacre, and the only way Sasquatch could bear to watch our lead slip away was by peaking helplessly between his leathered fingers.

Our less-than-narrow defeat was neither quick nor painless, but eventually the clock had the decency to stop ticking, the buzzer kind enough to sound.

In the locker room, Coach rested a foot on the metal bleacher, droning on and on about how it wasn't anyone in particular's fault, how we "ladies" couldn't go blaming ourselves.

But we could. It was easy.

And in the rare moments when we weren't busy blaming ourselves, we were busy blaming Sasquatch's hamstring, certain that if only the trainer's Icy Hot/Vicks VapoRub magic cure-all could have healed him, then none of us would've had to witness what we had: that sulking, bewildered giant cramped in his too-tight uniform, shaking his head as Meadowbrook ran up the score.

✻　✻　✻

The basketball season ended, as did Sasquatch's perfect attendance at Wallerton High. After the Meadowbrook game, he began showing up for school a bit more sporadically, rarely completing an entire week without my spotting the empty desk in pre-calc. Since the season was over, Coach didn't much care whether he was there or not, but strangely, some of his teachers did. Though it was always pretty apparent if there were no eight-foot-tall hominids in the room, Mr. Hernhold made it a point to read his name from the roll at the start of each class.

"Sasquatch?" he'd call, peering over the tops of his glasses. "Has anyone seen Sasquatch?"

By mid-March, sightings became something of a rarity, something worth whispering about in the halls.

One day after English class, Mrs. Gerry called me over and said, "Arnold, do you know where Sasquatch lives?"

"I mean, I know the general direction," I told her, thinking back to all the times I'd seen him vanish into the underbrush after games.

"Well, do you think you'd be able to deliver this?" she asked, offering me a fresh copy of *Huckleberry Finn*, required reading to finish out the year.

I stared at the book without taking it.

"It won't bite, dear," she promised, placing it in my palm.

I slipped it into my backpack alongside my math and bio books, each day Huckleberry growing flatter beneath their weight.

A week later I realized that what I'd mistaken for a heavy backpack was actually my growing guilt. And since I didn't want Sasquatch failing English on my account, I decided to do what was asked of me.

One afternoon I loaded up with bug spray and an ice-filled water bottle and carved a path through the woods, following – to the best of my ability – the footprints he'd left behind.

It was about a forty-minute trek to the Winnebago, but when I finally got there, there was no mistaking it. There were huge dents in its sides and all the windows were covered with trash bags. A fifteen-foot TV antenna pierced the sky, and just beyond it, a screened door torn from its hinges. Though I couldn't see him, his musk was so pungent my eyes began to tear up. Instead of knocking, I held a few feet back, summoning the courage to take another step forward.

A sudden rustling from behind, and I turned to find him there, eyeing me curiously, a basketful of blackberries clasped tight to his chest.

"Um . . . hey," I gulped. "Nice place. I like your . . . trash bags."

He didn't answer, just reached deep into his basket, devouring a handful of blackberries.

"You get cable?" I asked, nodding to the antenna.

He opened his mouth, so I reached for the water bottle, tossed a few ice cubes onto his tongue.

"Anyway, I'm supposed to give you this," I said, handing him the book.

He reached out a gigantic hand to retrieve it, smearing berry juice all over the pages.

I smiled, nervous, then smacked a mosquito.

"Well, okay. I guess I'll see you around then. In class or . . . wherever."

He grabbed my water bottle, helping himself to the remaining ice cubes and offering me the basket in exchange.

I stared at the bug-covered berries, watching all those thoraxes mounting the fruit.

"Nah, I'm okay. Thanks, though. They look really fresh."

Shrugging, Sasquatch returned my water bottle before turning his attention to the book – examining it from all angles and fluttering pages as if searching for the way inside.

❋   ❋   ❋

I never could get a good sense of Sasquatch the student. Like I said, he had the quadratic formula nailed down pretty well, but I couldn't speak to his other subjects. I know his English skills weren't particularly strong because sometimes I'd spot him working through *Huckleberry Finn* with Mrs. Gerry after school, his gargantuan finger following along in the text. From the hallway, I'd watch his lips stumble over the words like speed bumps, Mrs. Gerry nodding supportively while he waded through our language. Maybe he was a *Huckleberry Finn* fan, or a Mrs. Gerry fan, but whatever the reason, after my visit to his Winnebago, he began gracing us with his presence at Wallerton High with a bit more regularity.

Supposedly, he had a passion for shop class as well, and there was a rumor going around that he'd made just about the worst spice rack the world had ever seen, though Mr. Dillard – too afraid to comment while surrounded by Sasquatch and a surplus of buzz saws – simply gave him two thumbs up.

Quite proud of his handiwork, Sasquatch insisted on carrying that spice rack around with him everywhere he went, clutching it protectively to his hairy chest as he walked from Spanish to Art History.

"Got enough spices to fill that rack?" people often teased. "Plenty of dill? Got enough basil, Sasquatch?"

But Sasquatch knew better than to drag himself down to their level. He had a habit of smiling whenever there was even the slightest threat of confrontation, though admittedly, Sasquatch's smile was threatening in itself, the teasing typically halting the moment he bared his yellow teeth.

Maybe it was the spice rack (or the fur), but the girls paid even less attention to him than we guys did. That is, except for Becca Marsden who, toward the end of the year, took an unexpected fascination in him. She found him surprisingly alluring, often confiding in her female friends that she thought him the most "mature male" in the class. True, he was the only one among us with significant signs of facial hair, though it seemed an absurd indicator given his body hair.

Some days I'd catch Becca flash her smile at him in the hallway, or corner him in the locker room, staring up adoringly as she placed a tiny arm to his chest. Judging by his coos and purrs, I figured the feeling was mutual. It was love, almost, and while we assured ourselves that stranger things had happened, we had a hard time coming up with examples.

✳   ✳   ✳

Prom season hit like an epidemic, girls driven to resort to never-before-attempted tactics in order to secure their dates.

"Hey, Squatchy," Becca called, playfully slamming him against the lockers one day after gym class. "Listen, if you're not doing anything next weekend, maybe you wouldn't mind taking me, huh?"

Sasquatch stared blankly, then offered her his spice rack.

"No, I don't want that," she said, pushing it aside. "I want *you*. I want you to take me to prom. You know, the dance?"

She softened, bearing her own beautiful teeth. "So? What do you say?"

She leaned in close, allowing him full view directly down the front of her already low cut shirt. She smelled like flowers – an entire field of them.

"Well?" she repeated, running her nails through his fur. "What do you say, Teddy Bear?"

He nodded emphatically – *yes, yes, of course.*

Probably, he would've built her ten spice racks if she'd asked him.

"Great! Pick me up at 7:00?"

He nodded as she skipped off down the hallway.

And he continued nodding until I walked over to him, looked him straight in the eye and said, "Well, that was easy. Now the hard part's finding you a suit."

❉   ❉   ❉

But as we were soon to discover, that wasn't the hard part either.

Through some twist of fate, point guard Dave Malton had an uncle who owned the big and tall store over on Fourth Street. Apparently the man didn't get a lot of requests for size 40 × 60 pants, so he let us borrow slacks and a coat free of charge.

"It's for this basketball star," Dave explained to his uncle. "It's kind of his first date . . . ever."

Logistically speaking, there were other complications far more difficult than acquiring an enormous pair of slacks. For instance, we soon realized that Sasquatch was much too big to squeeze into any conventionally-sized car, and while there was some discussion about sprawling him in the back of a limo or flatbed truck, we eventually decided he and Becca would be most comfortable riding along with me and my date in the back of my father's convertible.

One problem solved, though the more difficult complication involved feet. It had been hard enough tracking down a pair of basketball shoes, but stumbling across dress shoes in Sasquatch's dimensions was virtually impossible. Thankfully, power forward Lester Freeman's mother was a master seamstress – she'd been hemming our dress pants for years – and for six sleepless nights she manned the sewing machine, extending a normal pair of hush puppies into gigantic leather canoes.

"They're not perfect," a red-eyed, hair-frazzled Mrs. Freeman admitted as she hefted them to Sasquatch, "but hopefully they'll do the trick."

One day after school we all headed over to Lester's house to watch Sasquatch model the whole ensemble.

"Not bad," Dave Malton nodded. "And hey, if that doesn't get her in the sack, nothing will."

But we knew better than to believe it.

At one point or another, we'd all endured the unfortunate experience of glimpsing a wet-furred Sasquatch showering after practice, and we remained confident that if the suit and shoes didn't get Becca Marsden "in the sack," his anatomical abnormality ("scientific miracle" as Dave called it) would probably prove successful. We were equally amazed and horrified by Sasquatch's member, perhaps more so than our actually spending time with Sasquatch himself. The guy made it hard for us to compete on a number of fronts. He already had the height advantage on the basketball court, and after the shower sightings, it became abundantly clear that he had the length advantage, too. I admit, the idea of Sasquatch laying Becca on a bed of roses made us uncomfortable, as if rendering all our own future sexual conquests somehow irrelevant. Still, he was our friend, or at least our Sasquatch, and what better way to boost the team's morale than to sacrifice what we loved most?

Sasquatch eyed himself in Lester's full-length mirror, as if he too had trouble recognizing the dapper (albeit fur-covered) gentleman staring back. Suddenly there was a new air about him, a slight panache deserving of any basketball star, though we didn't think he'd adapt to it so quickly.

"Got a couple burrs," I said, picking at his fur. "Lester, does your mom have a brush or something?"

"My dog does," he said, rushing down the stairs to retrieve it.

Since we'd all managed to survive the previous year's prom-related traumas, we figured ourselves experts on the subject.

"Now you're going to want to open the door for her," Lester coached.

"Right, and pull back her chair," Dave added.

"And be nice to her parents."

"And pick up the check."

"And get someone to help you with those cufflinks."

As I picked out the burrs, Sasquatch appeared suddenly woozy, as if he'd been the target of a few well-placed tranquilizer darts.

"You got all that, Big Boy?" Dave winked, clapping his shoulder.

Prom was still over a week away, but that didn't prevent Sasquatch from staring at me with the most mournful eyes imaginable. It was as if – despite our efforts – he was already acutely aware of the certainty of his extinction.

✳   ✳   ✳

After we endured the awkward photo shoot at Becca Marsden's house – "Sasquatch, you mind crouching a little lower? I want to be sure I have you in the frame," – we whisked our dates off to a steakhouse where I paid for everything with my father's credit card. Sasquatch's lifelong career of hunting and gathering hadn't converted into much in terms of U.S. currency, but he offered me a few pinecones and berries and a trout, so we decided to call it even.

"Thanks again for the lovely corsage, Sasquatch," Becca repeated as we walked back to the car.

It *was* a lovely corsage, and one that had set me back $17.00 (three pine cones and a trout after the conversion rate).

But the truth was, I felt awfully good about being able to give him the prom he deserved, and judging by the enormous erection floating around his trousers, he was feeling pretty good, too.

I couldn't blame him; we were talking about Becca Marsden after all. My own date, Jenny Rabin, was an incredible girl in her own right – my faithful, metal-mouthed girlfriend of two years – but all the hairspray, make-up, and push-up bras in the world couldn't transform her into Becca.

Becca in her peach-colored strapless dress.

Becca with breasts like balloons.

A goddess. A vision. Someone fit for magazine covers other than *Orthodontia Illustrated.*

Throughout the week, I'd done all I could to catch Sasquatch up to speed on all things prom-related. We'd dedicated an immeasurable amount of time on "date etiquette," and while he now knew the proper procedure for ladling Becca a cup of punch, it didn't occur to me until we entered the gymnasium doors that he didn't yet have the slightest clue how to dance.

After hours of arbitration, the illustrious and all-powerful prom committee had settled on the "Under the Sea" theme, and the walls were coated with what appeared to be blue plastic wrap, cellophane seaweed, white lights blinking up and down the walls like tiny bubbles.

I could hardly pay attention to any of it, far too preoccupied with Sasquatch's initiation into the brutality of high school romance.

"Want to dance, Teddy Bear?" Becca asked, pushing back her hair. Sasquatch looked to me for guidance, wondering whether he was supposed to get her the punch like we'd practiced, or, as Dave Malton had coached, if he was supposed to take her into the back of the Winnebago.

"She wants you to dance," I repeated, demonstrating a few moves myself. He imitated my one-foot shuffle, though his actions only managed to magnify my own uncoordinated efforts.

She rolled her eyes, so he stroked the front of her face with his palm as nature dictated.

"Hey! Don't be a brute," she joked, reaching for her compact and eyeing herself in the mirror. Upon spotting the damage he'd wrought she turned serious. "Damn it, Squatch. You smeared my foundation."

We watched her stomp into the bathroom, trailed by her entourage, and when she finally returned ten minutes later she didn't return to us.

Becca – who had found Sasquatch so endearing just minutes prior – was quickly tiring of his inability to be a proper date. Upon their return, we wandered back within face-petting distance of our dates, though this time – rather than continuing where he'd left off – Sasquatch began massaging Becca's scalp, instead. She started shooting S.O.S. looks to her friends; the message received by all the homo sapiens in the room.

"Maybe you want some punch?" I asked Becca, hoping to get Sasquatch back on track or at least momentarily out of her hair. She shrugged as if she didn't much care either way, so I started toward the punch bowl, Sasquatch trailing.

"Now look," I shouted over the music, watching as Sasquatch shoved through the punch line, leaving a few linebackers sprawling. "Becca's going to want to dance with you, so you're going to have to dance with her to keep her happy, does that make sense?"

He was so preoccupied fitting the ladle into his gigantic palm he didn't hear a word I said.

"Dance," I repeated, sashaying. "Think you can do that?"

Ignoring me, he kept his attention on fishing out the ice cubes as if they were wild trout.

"Okay," I said, grabbing his wrist, "nod once if you understand me."

He shrugged instead, his hands swallowing up the punch cups as we started back across the gymnasium floor.

But upon finding Jenny standing alone in the corner, braces glinting like a buzz saw, Sasquatch's confidence quickly subsided.

"What happened to Becca?" I asked her.

Jenny – who, on more than one occasion had said, "Arnold, if Sasquatch is so important to you, why not take him to prom?" – flipped her chin to the opposite side of the gymnasium. There, Becca stood engaged in what appeared to be a spellbinding conversation with her ex-boyfriend, Ed Gorman. Probably, he was apologizing for having felt her up prematurely, though in comparison to Sasquatch's face-petting/scalp-massaging, at least Gorman's groping seemed a bit more conventional.

Jenny clopped off herself, and I reasoned there wasn't much point in following.

Sasquatch and I planted ourselves firmly on the bleachers, a pair of downtrodden wallflowers with nothing but droopy boutonnieres. We knew this gym well, having hustled down every inch of it, but everything looked different when we weren't the center of attention.

Years later, I'd return to that gym and find myself still haunted by the memories. All those missed free throws, lay-ups. The three-pointer from the top of the key. The jump shot. The other jump shot. How I pulled instead of passed. Ducked instead of dribbled.

But there were other regrets, too: wishing I'd found the nerve to ask out all the girls I hadn't. Wishing I'd unfastened the push-up bra when I had the chance, smeared the make-up, run my hands through a girl's perfect hair. Wishing also that I'd applied to schools, sent out game tapes, tried walking onto a team or two.

But I didn't, not ever, and as the years slipped away I just grew older, fatter, and accepted my place on the bleachers alongside everyone else.

Thankfully, on prom night, Sasquatch and the rest of the team managed to hold the future at a safe distance, boxing it out the best we could as the precious minutes of youth wound down. While most of the guys made it a point to stop by and tell Sasquatch how damn good he looked in that suit coat, those shoes, it didn't seem to shake him from his stupor. Breaking up was hard – I would learn myself a few weeks later – and not even Sasquatch's freshly combed coat provided adequate protection for his heart.

Two slow songs and a chicken dance later, I glanced over to catch Sasquatch's curled fingers fiddling with a loose cuff-link while Frank Sinatra's "The Way You Look Tonight" wafted through the air.

"Here," I sighed, taking hold of his hand and placing it on my knee. I rolled his sleeve down his hairy arm, inserting the metal piece back into its fitting. He didn't pay me the slightest attention, his eyes still focused curiously on the lovely Becca as she folded herself back into her ex.

"All right, we got to get out of here," I told him, standing to leave.

He didn't shift his gaze.

"Hey, Sasquatch," I repeated, louder this time "it's time to hit the road."

Eventually, Sasquatch conceded, ducking beneath the balloon arch before following me to the parking lot where some of the guys had gathered around one of the cars, passing a couple bottles between them.

"Yo, Sasquatch," Lester cried drunkenly, his tie dangling from his neck, "you thirsty or what?"

He was, apparently, and from that moment forward we referred to that evening as "The Night Sasquatch Got Soused on Peppermint Schnapps and Nobody Could Blame Him." After all, if any of us had blown it half that badly with Becca Marsden, we would have done the same, probably worse, resorting to paint thinner or turpentine if necessary, anything to help us forget. In a show of solidarity, I matched him drink for drink, guzzling all kinds of throat-burning liquor in that silent parking lot, trying to ease our heartache.

The other guys must have thought us hilarious, wrapping our lips around the bottles like a couple of nursing babies. We just drank until we could hardly stand, then took turns trying to climb the wildcat statue just beyond the parking lot lights. Somewhere between Dave riding the wildcat like a bucking bronco and Lester chipping his tooth on the statue's tail, Sasquatch began his slow bumble back toward the woods.

"Hey, Sasquatch," Dave called, spotting him. "Where you headed? We gotta return that suit or my uncle's gonna flip."

Sasquatch stripped down right there in the parking lot, removing the enormous pants, the button-up, the suit coat. He even placed his specially made shoe canoes neatly beside the cufflinks.

I stumbled after him, following him to the edge of the woods but no further.

"Ey, maybe I'll see ya around," I slurred. "Whatya think?"

He shrugged, leaning against a tree as he doubled-over, vomiting a river into the leaves.

"That's what ya think, huh?" I laughed, balancing against a nearby tree myself. "Well anyway . . . anywho . . . we'll see ya around, huh? Won't we? Won't we be seeing you around, Sasquatch?"

He lumbered toward me, placed his palms on my shoulders, and nodded.

For a time, I actually believed him.

❋　❋　❋

Looking back, there are plenty of other regrets; it's the curse of retrospection.

But mostly the guys I still keep in touch with, we just keep rehashing our senior year's basketball season – its ups and downs, our untimely loss against Meadowbrook. Sometimes we dedicate entire evenings to discussing how things might have turned out differently.

But no matter how many times we replay it in our heads – sticking one second more on the shot clock, one final release at the buzzer – the score never changes, nor do we come to new conclusions. We're left knowing just what we always knew; that Coach was right, the only way we could've pulled off that win was with a healthy Sasquatch.

He was a biological curiosity, sure, but we on the team always knew he was also something more.

"A class act," Dave once proclaimed during a lunch break at the auto parts store where he works.

"Played ball with heart, too," agreed Lester who now steams carpets for a living.

Here in Wallerton, all that remains of Sasquatch are our weakening memories: a blurry yearbook photo, an empty space in the trophy case. Somewhere in my basement, there's a pair of 26EEE-sized shoes, but I couldn't tell you where.

We're not alone in our regret; Becca Marsden's runs much deeper. After dropping out of college, Becca married a long-distance trucker, though they soon divorced after her husband decided his top priority was driving microwaves to Salinas, California. We figured this had all been in the cards for quite some time. She put on a couple of pounds, woke one morning to find cellulite clinging to her thighs, and can now be found working part-time at the public library shelving mysteries. I've been told she's the proud owner of seven cats and enjoys making gingerbread houses. Rumor has it she dabbles in scientology.

People swear that some nights – when she's not at the library – her silhouette can be seen on the ridge overlooking the town. She's hollering into the woods, begging Sasquatch to return to her, shouting to all who will listen that her prom-night behavior was the biggest mistake of her life.

Despite my efforts, I've been unable to track him down myself. Old Sasquatch seems simply to have vanished into our past, a shadow of a memory. I've searched for him on every basketball court and in every Winnebago in the state. Every Dumpster. Even combed the woods behind the old high school, shaking a bag full of Big Macs.

I've looked under rocks, in caves, in the streams where the fattest trout swim.

Listened for the cracking of ice cubes.

Sniffed for his stench.

But the closest I've come are a few muddy footprints and an empty bottle of schnapps.

Westward Expansion

Manifest Destiny, Dad explained, is something we should always keep in the forefront of our minds. "Because the only reason California even exists right now," he chided, "is because our ancestors made it so." He nodded when he said this, walking my sister and me over to the scotch-taped map on the wall to trace the route the Fowler family trod while doing their part for American expansion.

On Dad's orders, Samantha and I would then shut ourselves in the computer room and play *Oregon Trail* in order to develop a better sense of our family heritage. Dad was adamant about our making use of this "learning aid," often dropping by to check on our progress, see if we had yet reached Fort Hall or the outpost. Sam – a third grader at the time – didn't yet know much of wagon trains, though this hardly discouraged her from arguing endlessly with me about how many axles and boxes of ammunition were required to survive the trek. Dad listened quietly from behind our computer chairs, though on occasion, the temptation to correct us proved too great. Once, when Sam and I decided to ford the river rather than take the ferry, our frustrated father informed us that fording a river was a "damn good way to come down with a bout of cholera."

"Haven't I taught you kids anything?"

When Dad wasn't lurking, Sam and I turned our attention to hunting buffalo, clicking the mouse as fast as we could to bring the hairy beasts down. Once, Dad walked into the room mid-bloodbath, crying out, "Jesus, guys. Never shoot more than you can carry home. We're not barbarians!" But we were, kind of, and although there were deer and rabbits to shoot, we knew better than to waste precious ammo on species that yielded so little.

"You know, historically speaking," Dad once explained, "the hunting aspect of the game is all wrong. Back in the good old days, pioneers were still reliant on the single shot muzzle-loaders. No way in hell a man could reload as fast as you're shooting – not even someone as skilled as your great-great-great-uncle Floyd. Common sense tells us that, and history."

Yet we continued to break the rules of history – clicking fast, killing often. We figured our great-great-great-uncle Floyd would've been proud – no one ever went hungry in our camp. While spinning in our chairs, Sam and I munched the limbs off animal crackers and waited for the buffalo stampede. The moment their pixilated bodies invaded our screen, we'd play our white man part to drive them to near extinction.

Click. Pow. Click. Pow. Ten thousand pounds of meat.

Mom didn't approve of any of this.

"I don't care who our ancestors are, that doesn't give you the right to shut our kids in a room all afternoon!"

"First off," Dad countered, "it's only for an hour or two every few days – a pretty minimal investment given the educational return. And second, once they manage to reach the ocean without wiping out half the goddamned wagon train, then they're free to take a break."

Sam and I could often be found listening from the other side of the door – a fact Dad knew well when he swung it wide.

"Right guys?" he asked, looking at us. "Tell your Mom. Am I right or am I right?"

We didn't know. All we knew was he was our father.

❋   ❋   ❋

There were things about Dad that Mom said if our teachers found out, we'd have child services swarming all over the house. Things like Dad's habit of leaving slabs of rotting meat in the basement sink. Things like the deer carcass splayed out in the living room for four days last November.

That year, Dad transformed himself into a mighty hunter, and though he initially appeared childish in his oversized orange vest and camo hat, the rifle added an unexpected legitimacy to the charade.

"Yup, off to bag some big game to feed the family," he said, insisting that we line up at the door to see him off. He liked to give the illusion that he was headed off to war, not just the backwoods off of U.S. 20.

And though we had our doubts, Dad turned out to be a pretty good shot, taking his deer during the season's weekend opener, even snagging a turkey a few months later.

Dad's friend, Ron Carter, was a fellow hunter, and a man who ran a deer farm to support the small faction of hunting tourists who lingered within the city limits. Mom thought the entire operation repulsive – to raise an animal only to shoot it for sport – but Dad explained it to us in terms we could understand: "It's called the Circle of Life. You saw the movie, right?"

Ron's industry made him nothing short of a venison aficionado. He ate deer the way most people ate chicken – in a seemingly endless array of possibilities. During his hunting years, Dad managed to try out nearly all of Ron's recipes: deer patties, deer stew, chuck wagon venison, even venison stroganoff. Dad made a production out of each of his so-called "creations," gathering us around the kitchen table for a sermon-length prayer, thanking God and the bullet and the deer and his steady hand. For theatric effect, he kept his meal veiled under a silver cover, leaving us to guess what peculiar concoction festered beneath.

Beaming, he'd say, "Without further adieu," and then, with a flourish, remove the cover. We'd look at it hesitantly, and hesitantly, he'd look back at us.

"Well, Ron gave me the recipe," he'd shrug, shaking his head. "Goddamn Ron. I didn't think it would even turn out as well as it did. It's a miracle, really."

Over the years, my father discovered that the problem with killing large mammals was space; that is, where you keep the carcass. Where *do* you keep a quarter hind? Ron Carter had recommended several butchers, but Dad – who fancied himself "one with the earth" – wanted to do it his way: "We shall honor this deer's untimely death by dividing her equally between the living room and basement sink."

This alternative to butchering practices was not embraced by all, though my mother, who had long before learned to pick her battles carefully, turned to Sam and me and said, "Please don't tell your teachers."

Before I could offer my own two cents, Dad and Ron had already begun dragging the front half of her into the living room atop a bloodstained tarp. She stunk of guts and wet leaves, though my father informed us that what we really smelled was victory.

We turned to our mother for answers.

"It's only temporary," she promised. "Just a day or two."

We kept staring.

"Look, he means well. He just doesn't know how to *be* well. Does that make any sense?"

Sam and I nodded because it was easier than continuing the discussion.

As Dad and Ron began filling the basement sink with her hindquarters, Sam and I took turns flipping through television channels, growing ever more uncomfortable with the third set of eyes watching with us.

❋   ❋   ❋

That year in sixth grade social studies, Mrs. Powell sent a letter home asking if Dad would like to give the class a short presentation on "the perils of westward expansion." We were just wrapping up the unit, and she'd been impressed by my knowledge of Manifest Destiny, the Kansas-Nebraska Act, and in particular, my analysis of the painting Dad kept in his den, the one called *American Progress*.

"Basically it's got this giant woman walking west with a book in her hand," I described to the class. "And all around her, families are in wagons and on horses, and they're all moving west, too. But the thing that most people don't see, the thing that my dad had to point out to me, was that the white woman is stringing telegraph wire as she walks. It's supposed to represent progress, I think, like the spread of progress to the west."

With that, quite regrettably, I'd piqued Mrs. Powell's interest and proved my father a credible source.

"Max, do you suppose your dad would be willing to speak to our class?" she asked one day after the bell rang. I knew the answer – *Yes! Certainly! Where do I sign up?* – but I shrugged and said he was usually pretty busy managing the line at the tire factory. "He works a lot of hours," I explained. "And this is their busy season. Tire season."

"Tire season, of course," she winked. "Well, maybe we'll try him all the same, see if we can't get lucky."

Mrs. Powell must have sensed my hesitation because she didn't ask me to deliver the letter directly. Instead, it arrived in the mail (making it more difficult to intercept), and Dad, who rarely received anything that wasn't a bill or a renewal request for *American West Quarterly*, made a grand production over the letter.

"Well what do we have here?" he called, extracting a rarely used letter opener from his desk and tearing the top off the envelope. He began reading it aloud, and from where I sat next to my sister on the couch, I could just make out his delighted facial expressions through the doorway to the den.

"Hey Maxy," he called to me. "You know any Cynthia Powell?"

"Social studies teacher."

I kept my focus on the television.

"Says here," he cleared his throat, "that she's selected *me* to give a presentation over at your school next week."

"Just a small talk, I think, Dad. And not for the whole school, just our class."

"Mmhmm. A presentation. Some kind of speech, it says here. On the perils of westward expansion."

"Maybe for like ten or fifteen minutes."

"Mmhmm. Well, I do know quite a bit about perils."

I glanced over to catch him drawing his finger blindly along the calendar. "Well let's see if I've got any openings . . ."

A few minutes later, I overheard him and Mom discussing it in the kitchen.

"I don't know, Amy. I'd have to take off work," Dad said, ho-humming around for Mom's permission. "It's just that I've been selected and all, and I'd hate to deprive the youth of America from such a valuable learning opportunity . . ."

"Just . . . try not to embarrass him," Mom whispered. "He's your son. Twenty minutes tops, okay? Tops."

He said sure, sure, of course, twenty minutes. A twenty-five minute presentation would be just about right. Maybe thirty, he assured, but not a minute more.

✳   ✳   ✳

I didn't tell anyone he was coming. Maybe, I thought, the class wouldn't even recognize him beneath his cotton smock.

I entered Mrs. Powell's classroom a few minutes early, and though he hadn't yet arrived, I could sense a kind of father-son-impending-doom in progress.

The others wandered in, slid into desks, anxiously awaiting the "surprise guest" Mrs. Powell had promoted throughout the week.

"As you all know," Mrs. Powell began, clasping her hands together, "today is a very special day for us. So special, in fact, that we've brought back a man who lived over one hundred and fifty years ago!" She waited for an awe that did not come. "And he made a trip all the way to the present day to tell you about a little something called . . . The Oregon Trail."

Jesus, I thought, *Dad put her up to this. He probably wrote her lines.*

From behind, I heard the clip-clop of dusty boots, a familiar clearing of the throat. The others turned, but I didn't; I knew what I'd see if I did.

"Has any of you's all seen Chimney Rock?"

I glanced up to view him in full garb, a hand blocking out the invisible sun as he scanned the faces of my peers. "Well, has you or ain't you? You ain't slow in the head, are ye? Answer me!"

On our family vacation a few years back, while driving through Oregon City, Oregon, Dad insisted we stop at some pioneer museum so he could show off his Floyd Fowler impression to the curator. The curator had listened thoughtfully as Dad recited his lines from memory. When he'd finished, Dad struck a heroic pose – knee bent and hands thrust toward the heavens – waiting for applause.

"Well," the curator had said, "that certainly was a liberal interpretation of pioneer colloquialisms. But you know, primary sources indicate that the language you have employed here, in particular the use of 'ain't' and . . . was it 'you's all'? In any event, those phrases are anachronistic of the time period, and further . . ."

Our red-faced father had no idea what the hell the man was talking about (he understood only that the guy wasn't clapping), so he stormed out, grabbing my sister and me by our hands as Mom followed close behind.

It was a tough lesson, though Dad's classroom performance served as proof that he'd taken none of it to heart. However, thanks to a more forgiving audience, his reenactment of Floyd Fowler received an encore from my classmates. Dad did everything from demonstrating how best to slather on bear grease ("Nature's bug spray!") to how to carve an apple with a Bowie knife ("Nature's carver!").

"You see, the thing most of you folks from the twentieth century don't realize," he said, clouds of dust puffing from his boots, "is that we pioneers didn't have all those newfangled contraptions you have nowadays. If we want fire, by God, then we rub some flint together and we make fire."

"Can you make one right now?" asked Jimmy Goings.

"Son, I'm glad you asked that," Dad smiled, pulling a pair of black shards from his pocket. "It would be my pleasure."

He began slapping the flints together, reaching for a few nearby geography tests for kindling. Mrs. Powell started a round of applause to signal the end of his performance, though my father missed the majority of his praise – far too preoccupied showering sparks to the pages.

"The damn... things... just won't light," he grunted, continuing his flicking. "What kind of paper you use here? Won't work if it's not pulp based, you know."

But apparently it was, because a moment later a slight crackle began curling at the edges of Jimmy Goings's D–. Jimmy began to cheer, then put his pinkies in his mouth and let out a wolf whistle.

Mrs. Powell reached for a nearby squirt bottle, extinguishing the flame prior to setting off the fire alarm.

"Now why'd you go and do that for?" Dad asked, scratching his head.

"All right then," said Mrs. Powell. "Let's give one more big thank you to Max's father." The class shouted a rousing thank you (especially Jimmy) as Floyd Fowler sauntered away.

"Well, you's all take care now," Dad called as he left the classroom, tousling my hair as he passed.

❋   ❋   ❋

The school year wound down, and much to my surprise, at closing ceremonies I received a commendation for physical fitness. I didn't win the *actual* award, but I was commended for *almost* winning the award. When my gym teacher, Mr. Dorchester, called my name, I rose unsteadily, accepting my certificate and verifying that the name on the paper matched my own. Dad gave me an embarrassingly long standing ovation, shouting, "Now that's a Fowler for ya!" until Mom yanked on his sleeve enough to settle him.

That night, I placed the certificate on my desk, but Dad insisted we get it framed the following day.

"No way in hell we're leaving a trophy like that unprotected from the elements."

"It's just a certificate, Dad . . ."

"Yes sir, my son the athlete," he said, holding the certificate at arm's length, admiring it from a distance. "Say, maybe we should sign up for the games this year?"

"What games?"

"What games? Hell, the Pioneer Games. In Weston. At the reenactment. Just a month away, you know," he said, tapping my head with his finger. I did know. Dad had highlighted the weekend of June 25th–27th on the calendar sometime last December.

The Weston Wagon Train reenactment had become a family tradition over the past few years, by which I mean my family traditionally endured it. The Pioneer Games, however, was one portion of the weekend from which I always kept my distance.

"We can start some kind of high intensity training regimen, if you're interested," he explained. "I've been watching the games over the last couple years. Mainly, it's just a lot of wood chopping and knot tying, the basics. Things you'd be good at."

I doubted it.

"So? Are you interested?"

I said probably not.

"*Probably,*" Dad repeated, replacing my certificate on my desk. "Well, we can certainly work with probably."

❋   ❋   ❋

In an effort to buoy my interest in the Pioneer Games, Dad began leaving less-than-inconspicuous stacks of wood scattered around the lawn. And also, an axe. And also, knotless ropes.

"Honey," Mom started in on him, "I just don't think it's safe to leave an axe lying around like that. What if one of the neighbor kids chopped off a foot?"

"Then the neighbor kids would learn a valuable lesson on trespassing, wouldn't they?" he countered. Dad had grown grumpy as a result of my unwillingness to be a contender and was apparently taking it out on the feet of our neighbors' children.

"You just have so much natural talent," he often reminded me. "Pioneer blood and everything."

In the mornings, while he went off to his managerial duties on the tire line, I wandered around the neighborhood and met up with friends so we could wilt our days away in pools and malls and everything unrelated to a life of hardship and tuberculosis.

But over breakfasts of scrambled eggs, Dad would regularly shove a fork into the food and announce the countdown until the Weston Wagon Train Reenactment.

"Twelve days," he'd say, then point a fork at me, sputtering eggs as he spoke. "It's not too late to start training." I'd nod, then excuse myself to the day's activities – more pools, more malls, less cholera.

Despite the enthusiasm gap between us, Dad maintained a grueling pace for his own training regime. In the wee hours of the morning, I'd sometimes catch him donning underwear and a t-shirt, rehearsing his Floyd reenactment in the basement where he thought we couldn't hear.

"We in the wagon train," he said, pacing about, glancing at himself in the mirrors, "we'd form circles around the fire at night, then put men on watch to protect us from the savage Blackfoot Injuns. They was known for their cruelty, ya know? They was even known," he started, then held a dramatic pause, "to scalp!"

I'd stand at the top of the stairs and listen to these lines repeated again and again. And I wondered, optimistically, if the addition of pants and a smock might add validity to his words.

✳ ✳ ✳

According to some sources, the Donner Party weren't the only pioneers to resort to cannibalism. In fact, at a family reunion a few years back, Great Aunt Gloria mentioned having heard of Floyd's own "crimes against nature" (recounting the tale in full while devouring a chicken leg). However, even after Dad received partial confirmation from our hearing-impaired Great Uncle Frank ("Who ate the what now?"), he was always careful to omit that part of Floyd's sordid past from his reenactments.

"Look Maxy," he said prior to beginning part two of his Circle of Life lecture. "Whether it's true or not, we all make mistakes, you got me?"

I nodded, he nodded back, and as far as he could tell, there was no need for further discussion. "Good. Well all right then," he said, placing his rough hands on my shoulders. "So let's not try to judge too fast or say too much, huh? It's not good to spit on skeletons."

Dad carried around his secret knowledge like a weight, the possibility haunting him. Sometimes, I'd find him dozing in the computer room, the words "cannibalism" and "Westward Expansion," placed side by side in a Google search bar like two very distant cousins.

This information prompted Sam and me to revise our *Oregon Trail* strategy. When we found ourselves out of ammo early on, we'd usually just starve ourselves so we could restart and begin the hunt anew. We'd watch our food supply dwindle, allowing those in our wagon train to die off one by one.

"You know, you could always just eat the kids," Sam whispered, cupping her hand to the pixilated people onscreen. "It seemed to work for Floyd Fowler."

WESTON, MISSOURI, 1846

It is not 1846, though for the weekend, we pretend it is.

Dad drove the station wagon the one hundred and twenty miles to Weston, and then, on arriving just outside the city, insisted we get into costume at a rest stop near the park.

"When we roll up there with all the others I want to look *authentic*," he said, stressing the word as he walked anxiously toward the bathroom, his arms loaded down with his costume.

In total, there were eight Conestoga wagons at the Weston Wagon Train Reenactment, along with eight families to fill them.

"We have been selected," Dad was always sure to remind us. "It's really quite an honor." Yet somehow, despite the rest of our family's utter disinterest, we kept getting selected again and again. A local ox herder loaned the reenactors the necessary oxen, and although Friday night was spent privately by those of us "selected" to be a part of the wagon train, Saturday was devoted to the spectators, with activities like the Pioneer Games, crafts, the wagon pulling demonstrations.

The only benefit of the Weston Wagon Train Reenactment was that it allowed my sister and me to see fanatics far more fanatical than our father. Like Stu Callahan, rumored to have recreated the entire trail in a covered wagon back in 1989. He'd written about it in *American West Quarterly*.

Stu greeted us before we could even unbuckle our seatbelts, shoving an authentically dirtied hand through our automatically rolled down window.

"Floyd," he smiled. "Glad to have ya join us on the trail."

While we were there, everyone always called our father Floyd. And much to our horror, the more people called him that, the more he grew into the part. By Saturday morning he'd already started wielding his gun and volunteering to take the first shift of guard duty to "ward off any of those injuns that might come a'lurkin'."

Ron Carter pulled up behind us in his truck and trailer – he and Dad spending much of Friday night in private talks in which our father tried recruiting him into becoming a "regular" in the "reenacting game."

"There's no other rush quite like it," Dad assured. "Not even drugs." And then, an afterthought: "Or sex."

Meanwhile, Mom tried to make friends with the other pioneer wives who'd been lured into the charade. Sam and I caught her and a few of the other women sneaking to somebody's car to flip through magazines and trade recipes for lemon meringue pie. Their husbands, too preoccupied with maps and figuring the best hypothetical route to the coast, failed to notice their wives' transgressions.

We children, who had become casualties as well, peered at our mothers longingly, questioning one another about the contraband we'd managed to smuggle back into the nineteenth century.

Friday night, Sam and I joined a few other kids for a swim in a nearby creek. Our fathers approved – it was an acceptable activity given the time period we were trying to recreate.

Thankfully, our fathers didn't see what we did there. As soon as we tromped out of sight, a pack of kids (myself and Sam excluded) reached for their cell phones and began chatting casually with their friends from the future. Rampant were phrases like "so lame" and "so boring" and "I'd honestly rather be dead" – words that had no place in 1846.

Sighing, I took off my authentic leather shoes and dipped my feet in the authentically cool stream. I kept expecting some bird to chirp overhead – this was nature, after all – but perhaps they'd caught wind of the reenactment and wanted no part in it.

"You signed up for the Pioneer Games?" asked Dennis Parker, dunking his feet beside mine. I recognized him from years past.

"Naw, I was thinking about it but . . . I just don't want to do anything that might make my dad proud of me."

"Yeah," he commiserated. "My dad forces me. But this time, if I win, he promised to take us to Orlando next year. My mom's making him. I think she's going to divorce him if he makes her wear any more bonnets."

"Yeah. Maybe my mom, too."

It grew darker, and when we returned to the safety of the wagon train, the cell phones turned silent yet again. We gathered around small fires, watching as our mothers prepared rabbit stew while our fathers set to work constructing the bleachers for the following day's festivities.

In his one breach of authenticity, our father – the weekend's Floyd Fowler – asked for a Phillips screwdriver, and a man begrudgingly handed it over so Dad could tighten the screws.

While standing alongside the popping fire, I viewed my father in a way I never had previously: as if after taking all the wrong trails, he'd at last landed in the proper time and place. A part of me was almost happy for him. A small part.

That night, we slept in the backs of wagons. Outside, the fires burned down while Sam, Mom, and I burrowed beneath blankets, using stuffed burlap sacks for pillows. From my place, I could see Dad's shadow creep along the ground alongside the others. The men chuckled deep into the night, debating issues related to twine and birch bark.

"I'll tell ya something about twine, though," Dad said. "It's damn near the most durable material you can imagine. Hell, I'd take it over sinew any day." The other shadows nodded.

"I mean that," he continued. "Show me a man with a spool of twine, and I'll show you one lucky man."

Sometime before dawn, I felt Dad climb in beside us, tug on the blanket, and adjust the burlap sack.

"Did I wake you?" Dad asked.

I grumbled.

"Sorry, pal," he said patting my head. "You just rest up for tomorrow."

❉   ❉   ❉

The following morning, when my name was ticked off the participant list as a "late addition to the Pioneer Games," I shot a look at my father who was busy pretending to polish his gun.

Helpless, I picked up an axe alongside boys like Dennis – boys who had things at stake – and at the sound of the whistle, I chopped as fast as I could, the blade sinking into the soft spot of the log. I split that wood over and over again, and even after the event concluded, I just kept hacking, turning it to pulp.

"Hey man," Dennis said, keeping his distance as the chips continued to fly. "Hey, we have to go tie knots."

I threw down my axe, watching as the other boys lined up, anxious to try out their cow hitch or their double figure eight.

"Dennis," I said, wiping my brow and starting toward them, "you think you could teach me a noose?"

* * *

After I lost the Pioneer Games (Honorable Mention), and after Dennis took second, Dad came up to both of us, placed a hand on each of our shoulders, and said we'd given it all we had.

"And where'd you learn to tie an oysterman stopper knot anyway?" he asked me.

I refused to look at him.

"Oh, come on," he said. "It's a growing experience! You forgive your old man, right?"

"Sorry, Floyd."

For the rest of that day, the bleachers were crowded with people equally as obsessed as my father. Often, when there was no performance or lecture, the audience was invited to participate in tutorials on soap-making, candle-making, even leather work. People purchased cups of rabbit stew from Mom, ate venison jerky, drank cups of fresh pressed cider while the apple skins rotted in thin circles on the grass. Cans of Budweiser were stashed in a cooler behind the wagons, though spectators were asked to drink their beers by the cars so as not to "compromise the integrity of the atmosphere."

For much of the afternoon, I ground teeth and cracked knuckles in the back of the Conestoga wagon. I watched men and women in sunglasses and button-up shirts peruse the grounds, ask the reenactors all about the kind of weight a wagon could hold, from what type of wood the axles were carved, the true importance of the yoke. Dad appeared to have the answers to everything and more, oftentimes positioning himself in the center of the circle while he employed his vast tire manufacturing knowledge to tackle any subject.

"The thing about yokes," he said, pressing a firm hand to an elderly man's shoulder, "is that there are two kinds: the bow yoke and the head yoke." Ron Carter stood behind him, nodding. "Most people don't know that, and it's unfortunate because . . ."

I turned away, watched Sam and my mother dipping candles into alternating bins of hot wax and cold water.

"Hey there, Max," Mom said, smiling at me. "Twenty-four hours and we can all go home."

"Did you know he signed me up?" I asked. Her smile wilted. She didn't answer, didn't say anything. Instead, she peeled wax from her hands, her fingerprints sticking. Sam re-dipped her candle once more.

"Ta-da" she called, handing me the gift. "For my brother, the honorable mention."

As night loomed the crowd settled back into the bleachers, preparing to watch us perform a short play on the hardships of pioneer life. This took much convincing. We kids were supposed to look sad and hungry and tired, and we'd been instructed to fan ourselves with our hands to show the heat we had to endure "day in and day out," as Stu Callahan, our director, explained. "Think you kids can handle that?"

I'd chopped wood, I'd tied knots. Yes, I could handle that.

Dad's part required him to blather on and on about the possibility of starvation, how the hunting just wasn't as good as in years past, how provisions were running low and food was beginning to spoil. It was the largest part and just the part he wanted. Mom's job was to knit and appear unobtrusive, which was just what she wanted, too.

The first ten minutes or so went smoothly enough, but then Dad cleared his throat, walked to center stage and began ad-libbing a few lines.

"Dear God," he called, arms outstretched before him. "Heavenly Protector! We need food to feed our families. We got lit'uns starving out here," – dramatic pause – "dying!"

The crowd gasped, then chuckled.

He paced to the other side of the platform. "We're sick and we're weak," he said, falling to one knee. He picked up his gun, eying it as if it might be the bringer of food. "Who will be the one to save us?"

I had a pretty good idea, but I wasn't going to watch him do it. I, too, was sick and tired, and my spirits were hardly raised by my father's efforts to upstage everyone else. As I watched him struggle through his routine it occurred to me that Dad wasn't acting at all; this was just him.

I walked off the front of the stage, and as Dad continued his speech about the "lack of sustenance," I mumbled, "You know, Floyd, there's always cannibalism."

My father froze, watched me take a seat in the bleachers alongside old men in American flag shirts. After a pause, he continued his carefully rehearsed lines. As he spoke, he leaned against his gun like a cane, chattering on as if nothing fazed him except, of course, the impending fear of starvation. I made fists, I counted to ten – both failed attempts at calming the pioneer blood within.

＊ ＊ ＊

It all became clear much later. How when Dad gave the signal – waving his gun in the air and shouting, "But the Lord will provide!" – Ron released one of his hand-fed deer from the back of a trailer and into the brush just behind the stage. Then Dad really put his theatrical skills to work, and much to the surprise of his fellow reenactors, pointed to the newly arrived deer and raised the gun.

"Glory to God! Sustenance!"

And then he blew her head off.

It was that quick. There was a head and then there was not one – just four legs buckling like an unhinged table, a torso corkscrewing into the ground. The horrifically hoofed tap dance elicited an array of reactions, most of them tinged with some form of gagging. Almost immediately, the man to my left began vomiting; nobody told him his reaction was historically inaccurate.

The deer stuttered one final step before wobbling to the dirt. Her chest fell first, followed by her hind, and then, the great thundering of a body at rest.

There was no trophy left worth mounting. Just venison.

"And the Lord hath provideth!" Dad shouted.

If there had been a curtain, this would have been an opportune time to close it. But there was none; just a crowd of horrified spectators trapped in the bleachers, screaming.

In yet another breach of authenticity, someone must've reached for a phone because within minutes – as Dad tried calming everyone down ("Don't worry, plenty for all!") – a DNR officer leapt from his jeep, gun drawn.

"Sir, I need you to drop that rifle right now."

There was so much noise, so much commotion, that almost everyone forgot about the deer carcass fifty yards away.

Dad dropped the gun, put his hands up.

"While I have done as requested," Dad began, "I'll have you know that I do not recognize the authority of the DNR. My name is Floyd Fowler, and the year is 1846 . . ."

"Sir! Get on your knees now."

"Hey, listen," Dad whispered, starting toward the ground. "I was just trying to make it authentic, all right, officer? Like how our ancestors did it. To keep from starving. This wasn't sport, okay? This wasn't a sport kill."

The crowd began to dissipate, mothers ushering their kids into the backs of Conestoga wagons while the men fumbled with their beards and suspenders, some making their way over to examine our father's kill. The ones that remained wrapped their arms tight around their families, promising never to return to this lunatic-ridden Godforsaken place.

"It's how it was done in the good old days," Dad repeated as he was pushed toward the jeep. "You have to understand this." His eyes glanced everywhere for help. "Right? Hey! Hey! Someone tell this guy that this was how it was done back then. That it's histori-cally accurate."

No one stood up for my father.

"Jesus, kid. The plan wasn't to kill it," Ron Carter told me, coming from behind. "Just pretend. We were supposed to be pre-tending. Reenacting."

The DNR officer shoved my father's slumped body into the backseat of the jeep.

"Back then, it was our destiny!" Dad shouted. "Our obligation!"

"Our Manifest Destiny!" I cried.

Our father had shot a deer out of season, and this, we were informed, was serious. Nevertheless, within a week's time, it was mostly resolved. Not better, just resolved. Dad paid the one thousand dollar fine and had his hunting license suspended for three years. Then, after a bit more paperwork, the state begrudgingly forgave him.

"Just be grateful he didn't get jail time," the DNR officer informed our mother. "You can get up to ninety days for a stunt like that."

But Dad wasn't grateful, and he certainly never referred to what he'd done as a stunt.

"The children were starving," he defended. "What other choice did I have?"

The following morning, when we'd returned home, the first thing Dad did was rip his *American Progress* print from the wall in his den. He crumpled it, said we Americans knew nothing of progress. Next, he tossed all of his carefully organized back issues of *American West Quarterly* into the trash can, mumbling something about "no longer wasting his time with that smut."

Never again did my father and I approach the subject of cannibalism of the nineteenth century. We just didn't. Not even when all the pixelated buffalo ran out and the computer game demanded it. That sordid chapter of our lives – we hoped – we'd left behind in Weston.

That night for dinner, Dad took what remained of last year's deer from the freezer and prepared his specialty – oven-barbecued venison. I watched him baste in silence. He turned around, saw me there, and told me to make myself useful: set the table with the good silverware.

"And get some placemats," he added. "The ones with the trim."

Then, we all sat around the table and waited for Dad to say grace, thanking God for his steady hand, etc. But he didn't. He just shoved the food toward us.

"Now look, we are going to finish this meat," he explained calmly, resting his hands on the table. "Is that clear?" Sam nodded, forking a piece and leading it to her mouth. Barbecue sauce dripped the return route to her plate, leaving behind a perfect trail.

Dad, his chair pushed back, sat solemn, watching us chew. We tried to pretend we enjoyed it. Throughout the meal, Mom continued commenting on how wonderful everything was.

"Mmm . . . so tender. And the silverware! And the placemats! Max, did you do this?"

I ripped into another hunk of venison, and, mouth full, gulped my milk glass empty.

"They're just placemats," I chewed, eyeing my father. "It's not like we're barbarians."

The Clowns

The Clowns moved in on a Thursday, two months after their son, Bubbles, perished in a cannon-related accident and just days after taking a devastatingly hard hit from the recession. On the advice of their financial planner, Mr. Bobo Longbottom, the Clowns had invested bullishly in seltzer water as the entertainment industry plummeted around them. Business slowed – people just didn't have a lot of money to throw around on clowns anymore – and due to the decline in birthday party performances and the rising costs of funerals, the Clowns found, one cold October day, that they could no longer pay their mortgage. The bank foreclosed on their home, and finding themselves with no place to hang their polka-dotted hats, they called upon my father.

They were second cousins, or something like that, and citing familial obligation, Dad said there was no greater honor than to assist them.

Mom and I were hesitant, though Dad rebuffed our concerns.

"The Clowns have dedicated their entire lives to bringing joy to others," he reminded. "The least we can do is try to give a little back."

I hardly knew them. They weren't regulars around the Thanksgiving table, and while they sent me my annual birthday card – "Wishing you a wacktackular birthday!" – that was the extent of our relationship. We'd gone to Bubbles's funeral, of course, though I'd kept my distance, sending sympathetic looks from afar, hoping they'd prove sufficient.

During the car ride over, when I asked Dad exactly how we were related to the Clowns, he referenced my Great Aunt Norma and then began using phrases like "twice-removed" and "half-sibling" until eventually he just sort of fizzled out completely.

"Good people, though," my father added. "Always have been."

They were a strange pair – perpetually in full clown regalia – and throughout the funeral service, every time Aunt Clown tried to wipe her nose a loud "honkahonka" permeated throughout St. Francis's Chapel, overpowering the organist and causing the priest to perpetually lose his place in the eulogy. Uncle Clown's grief was equally uncomfortable, and when Dad stretched out his arms to embrace him, Mr. Clown's plastic flower lapel sprayed a stream of seltzer directly into Dad's face. Dad was a good sport, and when Mr. Clown apologized and tried handing him a handkerchief, he discovered, quite to his horror, that the more he pulled the more handkerchiefs spilled out.

"Oh, damn it," Mr. Clown cried, pulling from various pockets, equally unsuccessful in finding a single, usable kerchief that wasn't part of a chain. "Oh, Christ."

I watched helplessly as he pulled and pulled, sending streams of colors floating through the air, making their slow descent.

"One second now," he told my father. "Let me just try this pocket. My God, this can't be happening. Of all the goddamned days…"

Those of us still in the pews glanced down at our watches or turned toward the wall, attempting to keep his embarrassment private.

It could have been quite funny if it weren't so tragically sad.

※　※　※

I don't have to describe them.

The usual.

Shoes ten sizes too big, enormous polka-dotted jumpsuits, gloved hands, painted faces, and bulbous red noses protruding. Red paint outlined their mouths, guaranteeing a smile, even in the shadow of death.

"Hey, Sophie," Dad called up the stairs to me on the day they moved into our house. "Go help your Aunt Clown with her things, huh?"

She wasn't my aunt, though "aunt and uncle" seemed the closest the branches of our family tree were willing to twist.

I stepped outside and helped Aunt Clown with her handbag, watching as Uncle Clown pulled trunk after trunk from their Volkswagen Beetle.

"Just a couple more now," Uncle Clown said, stacking their belongings three times as high as the car. Aunt Clown didn't say anything. She looked sad, even with that face paint.

Meanwhile, Uncle Clown was having a difficult time himself, particularly with navigating our narrow stairs while trapped in gigantic shoes. His arms were loaded with boxes marked JUGGLING

BALLS and HAND BUZZERS, but every time he made it halfway up his shoes betrayed him, sending him sprawling backward – classic slapstick.

He didn't say anything, just grimaced before wiping the sweat from his face.

"Let me help you with that," Dad offered, but Uncle Clown shook his head, ran a gloved hand through his curly, red afro and just leaned there against the wall.

Finally, in an attempt to break the tension, Aunt Clown pressed PLAY on a tiny, handheld tape recorder, and hyena laughter burst through the room.

The silence turned to smirks, the smirks to laughter, and soon we were all doubled over and feeling a whole lot better.

"Haha, very funny," Uncle Clown groaned, rolling his eyes. "She's got a great sense of humor, huh, folks?"

✳   ✳   ✳

We tried not to listen to their fights, though it was hard, especially with those enormous shoes tromping overhead. Dad reasoned their marital problems were likely the result of their financial woes compounded by the death of their son – a one-two punch they couldn't shake.

"I can't imagine," my mother kept repeating. "I simply can't imagine."

Every time we heard Uncle Clown bumbling down the stairs we went to great lengths to appear as if we hadn't heard a thing, returning our eyes to the television and feigning interest in whatever juicer the infomercial was peddling.

Uncle Clown never even acknowledged our attempts. He had gotten into the habit of helping himself to my father's liquor cabinet, clinking a few ice cubes into a tumbler, pouring the whiskey two cubes deep. Nobody ever mentioned it. Didn't mention the smell on his breath or his stumbles or when his humor just turned mean. Through it all, Aunt Clown continued wearing her lopsided smile, helping Mom prepare meals, doing odd jobs around the house.

"We're just... we're so grateful to be here," I'd overheard Aunt Clown whisper one night as she and Mom put away the dishes. "Surely business will pick up. We'll get a few birthday parties, maybe some corporate picnics . . ."

Mom had become an expert nodder, continually assuring Aunt Clown that they were no inconvenience, that they were welcome as long as they liked.

"Besides, it's nice to have a little laughter around the house," she tried, but she knew she'd said the wrong thing.

On the worst nights, after Uncle Clown downed his drinks he'd lurch back upstairs – "Just need to fix my face," he'd say before locking himself in the bathroom. I'd often be in my bedroom across the hall, working on homework, the door slightly ajar as I listened to the water pipes squeak. Twenty minutes later, when I heard the bathroom door click open, I couldn't help but watch his bulbous nose emerge from the steam, followed by the towel wrapped around his startlingly white waist, a near-perfect match for his face paint.

"Hey, Sophie," Uncle Clown once slurred, fitting a Q-tip into his ear with one hand while gripping the towel with the other. "You hear the one about the clowns and the cannibals?"

"Um . . . no," I said, putting down my pencil, my attempt at accommodating him.

"Long story short, the cannibals released 'em," he said, pausing, a wry smile pasted across his painted lips. "Claimed they 'tasted funny.'"

I didn't know what to do so I didn't do anything, just sat there, frozen.

He honkahonka-ed his nose and when that didn't work, said, "Ahhh, to hell with it. Everyone's a critic."

✳   ✳   ✳

This went on for a couple of weeks, everyone pretending as if everything was normal. I didn't say a word after I unclogged the shower drain of red hair, nor did I complain about the white face paint smeared on the table, marking the exact coordinates of where Uncle Clown most recently passed out.

Even the neighbors – who'd seen Bubbles's obituary in the paper – were kind enough not to make too big of a scene as they watched my drunken uncle attempt to mow zigzagged lines in our lawn in his squeaking 26EEE sized shoes. Likewise, the mailman took it upon himself to forward their subscription for *American Clown Quarterly* directly to our doorstep, and even the Jehovah's Witnesses managed to walk on past every time they spotted the red-nosed man passed out in the kiddie pool.

Yet despite their eccentricities, my parents were right, they were good people – at least good clowns – and Aunt Clown always offered to help wash dishes or set the table. And better still, she left intricate balloon animals on my pillow on the days she changed the sheets – a menagerie of latex walruses and white-handed gibbons greeting me every few nights.

Yet the Clowns couldn't stay cooped up in the house forever. Most mornings they'd load up their Volkswagen and tour the city, working the street corners, "prostituting ourselves," Uncle Clown often grumbled, "turning tricks for cash."

But it was more than that, more than simple tricks.

They actually made quarters leap from behind people's ears, pulled rubber chickens out of their armpits. They had the unique talent of juggling apples and oranges and pears all at once, as if they alone kept the universe in motion. In the evenings we'd all watch television while Uncle Clown – pre-nightcap – struggled through a few sets of push-ups. And other nights – post-nightcap – when he was feeling extra loose, he and Aunt Clown would sit us down in the backyard and put on their show.

They only had so many routines, but we clapped and cheered even at the ones we'd already seen. That handheld tape recorder played the same calliope music again and again, but we pretended we were hearing it for the first time.

"Sophie," Uncle Clown often gasped, his throat laced with whiskey. "What's that . . . quarter doing behind your ear?"

He'd remove it, of course, amid our clapping, and after his grand finale – involving a unicycle, six bowling pins, three shots of tequila, and a hula-hoop set aflame – he and Aunt Clown would take a knee, waving their hands in the air, perfectly synced with the music.

While Mom, Dad, and I wished they didn't feel the need to perform for us, we couldn't do anything to stop them.

"Look, just enjoy it," Uncle Clown begged, sweating like an iceberg. "It's all we know to do to pay the rent."

And then one day the water pipes burst.

A Sunday, after Uncle Clown had done two hundred push-ups the previous night in preparation for what he called his "reunion tour," which was actually just a brief appearance at Clarence Robards's eighth birthday party. Still, it was $50.00, and neither he nor Aunt Clown was in a position to pass it up. Mr. and Mrs. Robards had been quite clear in their expectations – "We don't want a lot of circus tricks," they'd informed him. "Just pull some quarters from their ears."

Thankfully, this was Uncle Clown's forte.

"Like riding a horse," Uncle Clown whispered, sitting me down in the kitchen that Saturday night as he practiced pulling all kinds of currency from behind my earlobes.

For a brief moment, everything seemed almost right in the world – people were laughing, money was falling out of my ears – but then we woke the next morning to find the bathroom pipes hissing sprits of water, the cold mist collecting across the tiles, covering the entire room in a slick glaze.

"This ship's going down!" Uncle Clown yowled, his idea of a joke. But when Dad came pounding up the stairs, he was less than thrilled by the water damage.

I stepped into the hallway to find Uncle Clown dancing in the spray, rubbing a scrub brush along his polka-dotted jumpsuit while singing "I'm so Excited" by the Pointer Sisters. Dad kept a hand pressed to his forehead and began counting backward from ten.

Aunt Clown witnessed the scene and urged her husband to stop the routine.

"Please," she begged. "This isn't a laughing matter."

"Yeah, you're right, hon," Uncle Clown said, laughing harder. "Because we've just had so many laughing matters lately, haven't we?"

Neither of them had to say anything.

They wore their pain on their polka-dotted sleeves.

Mom joined us next, and Uncle Clown started in on the second verse of the song while Dad fought his way toward the shower drain, reaching a hand into the grate. Water sprayed in all directions – a seltzer bottle gone berserk – but eventually Dad got the bright idea of turning off the water pump before tackling the drain head-on. He returned to the bathroom to find my uncle toweling himself off, his jumpsuit deflated under the weight of the water.

He was still bellowing: "You're not fully clean until you're Zestfully . . ."

"Please, stop," Aunt Clown begged, and while Uncle Clown tried to bite back his grin, his face paint refused to back down.

"So some pipes rusted through, big deal," Uncle Clown shrugged to my father. "Tell you what, I'll pitch in the fifty we get from the Robards gig, how's that? Fix'er right up. No sense crying over old pipes, am I right?"

"Not old pipes," my father grunted, tugging fistfuls of red hair from the shower drain. The pyramid continued to grow beside him, a floor mat's worth of Uncle Clown's shedding fur.

"Oh, so what? You're going to try to pin this on me?" Uncle Clown asked. "You think a few strands of somebody's hair are going to make pipes burst like that?"

"*Somebody's* hair?" Dad gasped, leaping to his feet and slamming the last chunk of red coils onto the edge of the tub. "Who the hell else around here has red hair?"

He had a good point – Aunt Clown's hair was blue.

"Oh, so now the man's a plumber," Uncle Clown laughed.

"And a barber, too, apparently."

"Look, I know you're going through a rough patch," my father began, "but please understand that we want to help you through any way we . . ."

"Oh, shove it up your . . ."

Anticipating his colorful language, Aunt Clown reached for her slide whistle, overpowering him with a single breath.

Nobody laughed at the sound.

"Now look here . . ." Dad gritted, stepping toward him.

"No, you look here," Uncle Clown countered, pointing to his flower lapel.

A stream of water squirted Dad in the eye, and this time, he was far less of a good sport.

Dad and Uncle Clown fought their way out of the bathroom, we three spectators shouting and pleading with them to stop.

Dad had my uncle in a chokehold, and soon they were somersaulting down the stairs, crashing into walls and shattering picture frames before returning to solid ground. They shook off the glass and leapt to their feet once more, Dad stomping on Uncle Clown's gigantic shoes, pinning him in place like a punching bag. My father absorbed the scattershot blows, but when he returned fire, he always aimed directly for Uncle Clown's nose, a high-pitched "honkahonka" erupting with each well placed punched. They rolled to the floor once more, their hulking bodies flattening the nearby whoopee cushions, farting sounds erupting, adding to the soundtrack that already included grunts and gasps and moans. I'd never seen my father fight anyone – he'd told me violence was barbaric – but suddenly there he was kneeing my uncle in the stomach, pressing the clown's chalk-white face into the wall.

"Say uncle," Uncle Clown gasped, though, twisted against the couch, he was in no position to call any shots. "Say uncle, damn you."

My father didn't, though eventually he relented, releasing my uncle from the chokehold without even making him say uncle.

Mom, Aunt Clown, and I were left to stare out at the destruction: empty seltzer bottles piled high, a unicycle half-crushed beneath a chair. Juggling balls were scattered like landmines, hand buzzers like brass knuckles.

It looked like some kind of face-painted massacre.

My father limped into the kitchen, returning with an ice pack.

"Hey, put some ice on that eye," he said, tossing the pack to my uncle. "Nobody's going to pay to see a black eye on a clown."

Uncle Clown caught the ice pack with one hand, nodding as he lifted it to his face.

"Hey," Uncle Clown called to him. "Thanks for not killing me back there."

He winked like he was joking, though his eyes appeared to have taken on some seltzer.

Dad nodded, then sifted through the mess on the floor until stumbling upon Uncle Clown's endless chain of handkerchiefs. He handed it over.

"Thanks, partner," Uncle Clown said, blowing his nose and releasing a solitary "honka."

Nobody said anything then – a silence so deep that even the whoopee cushions had the good sense to deflate inconspicuously.

As I stood there, watching my aunt press the ice pack to her husband's eye while Mom moved Dad to the den, I realized – with some comfort – that we were back to what we'd always been.

Not better, not worse – just a family in desperate need of a punch line.

Line of Scrimmage

This must have been seventh grade or so.

My father had just left to fulfill his dream of becoming an impressionist painter somewhere in the Vermont wilderness, and my football coach, Coach Housen, was busy telling us to "Whip their dicks!" and "Smack their asses!" among various other phrases that didn't make a lot of sense to those of us sitting in the locker room.

"You know what I'm talking about," Housen clapped. "I want you to get out there and slap those fannies like you mean it, really dig your shoulder in right around the groin. And here's the rub, boys: you gotta commit! Either commit or go home and nurse off your mother's teat. None of this pantywaist bullwonky. I want nothing less than long term commitment. Bend 'em over. Ride 'em cowboy style. Wrap 'em up and sink your teeth directly into their peters," he barked, snapping his teeth like a vise, crossing his arms.

"Any questions?"

We had about a million questions.

Why were we putting our shoulders into their groins?

Sink our teeth into their . . . peters?

"No questions? All right, hands in," Coach called. All thirty of us gathered round, our cleats clicking against the smooth cement. We piled sweaty hand atop sweaty hand.

"Okay. All together, now. Whip their dicks, on three . . ."

Housen was the harmless type. Bewildered, out of touch, but at the end of each practice he'd have us take a knee while he preached some on-the-spot sermon about what he'd witnessed out on the field that day. Something related to our dedication, our sacrifice, our grit.

"And remember," he concluded each sermon. "We win as a team and we lose as a team, but whatever the score, we'll always *be* a team."

Turned out what we did best was lose as a team.

After our stunning defeat against Central Christian (52–0), Housen lined us up on the end zone so that we might learn from our mistakes.

"I don't care if your parents *are* waiting in the car," he paced, his hands buried deep into his windbreaker. "No one's leaving this goddamn field till we learn how to play defense." We were mud-soaked and tired and cold. Shivering. Our shoulder pads weighed us down, our helmets cramped our ears.

"Yancey," he hollered to me. "Show us some defensive mobility, would ya?"

Some what? Did second string kickers even have that?

"Come on, Yancey, knock it off with the dillydallying."

Dillydallying?

I crouched on all fours.

"Like this, Coach?"

"Jesus, Yancey. Really?" he asked, throwing his hat to the grass. "Like this."

He demonstrated for me, clenching his fists and managing a slow rocking motion, his pelvis leading.

"All together now!"

We clenched our fists, tensing our buttocks and pumping forward from our crotches.

Housen nodded.

"Now we're getting it. Take it nice and slow. Sometimes you gotta go in for the tackle balls first. Lead with those hips, boys, lead with those hips. Don't be afraid to use those butt muscles."

We slow-humped the chilly September air until there was nothing left to hump. Humped, grunting, thrusting, thoroughly exhausted as the rain trickled down the glossy slope of our helmets.

After ten minutes or so of demonstrating defensive mobility, Hans Rochester, a back tackle, said, "Coach, I think we gotta go." He pointed to a crowd of bewildered parents gathering by the fence.

"Oh really? Well I know one place ya gotta go. To the fifty and back!" He blew his whistle. "Move it! I wanna see those tight asses shake."

Daryl Harbeck (second string ball holder) breathed heavily beside me.

"We could always just . . . quit," he gasped.

"Quit," I agreed. "Yes . . . we could do that."

But our dedication was simply too great.

❉   ❉   ❉

Nights after practice Mom and I sat down on the kitchen stools with a telephone book and began calling Vermont's local authorities.

Police stations, fire stations, the YMCA.

"Yes, hello. You haven't happened to notice a stranger in town? Frederick Yancey. About 5'9", sort of squat. He's a painter, you see..."

She was desperate for answers, so she made me desperate, too. Addison County hadn't seen him, nor had Caladonia or Chittenden or Essex.

We had some much-needed luck in Bennington, when a police officer recalled, "Well, there used to be some painter around here. What was his name?"

His name was Norman Rockwell.

Mom continually excused Dad for his actions, claiming that after fourteen years of forty-hour workweeks at the insurance firm, perhaps he deserved to momentarily cut all ties.

"We shouldn't worry," she assured. "I'm sure he'll be back in no time. Most men buy a sports car, for crying out loud," she laughed. "He'll come back to us, right, sweetie?"

One day, we just stopped calling Vermont all together. Still, Mom ordered phonebooks from neighboring states: New Hampshire, Delaware, and much of the New England region.

But even after they arrived, we didn't bother calling. We just stacked them on a shelf and used all the money we were saving on long-distance to order Kentucky Fried Chicken by the bucket.

"That crazy father of yours...he's just so...crazy," she smiled, licking her fingers. "Excuse me, Rexy." She pushed past me and locked herself in the bathroom.

I devoured a wing and then sat by the phone, in case Vermont called back.

❋   ❋   ❋

The school's annual Father-Son breakfast snuck up on everyone, and one day after practice, as we peeled ourselves out of our pads and hit the showers, Coach Housen loomed in the doorway staring at his clipboard.

After much towel slapping and six rounds of Goldbond powder fights, we dressed and left the locker room, our backpacks slung cockily over one shoulder. Coach Housen spotted me among the herd and shouted, "Yancey, office, pronto."

It wasn't much of an office – just a glorified janitor's closet with a desk and a lightbulb squeezed in beside the boiler. He'd cluttered it with things only slightly related to football. Back issues of *Sports Illustrated* piled haphazardly beside a microwave. A crossword puzzle. A half-finished maze on the back of a Denny's children's menu. Two coffee mugs, each proclaiming him the "World's Best Coach."

He leaned back in his green swivel chair, rocking gently.

"Yeah, Coach?"

He nodded, staying quiet for a moment, his forefingers forming a triangle in front of his lips. Finally, he spoke.

"Doing some good work out there, Yancey. Your kick's improving, and you're holding nothing back in terms of really butt munching the opponent."

How does one munch a butt?

Was I really good at it?

"Uh . . . okay, Coach," I nodded. "Well, thanks." I started out of the office.

"I mean that," he said, motioning me back. I leaned against the doorframe.

"You wanna take a seat, kid? You look restless."

"No, thanks."

He paused again, then nodded, leaning forward, adjusting the mugs on his desk.

"Ever seen mugs like this before?" he asked, pushing them toward me.

"Uh-huh. My dad has one. Only it says 'World's Greatest Dad,' I think."

"Well is he?"

I didn't say anything. Most of the school already knew he'd vanished, so I just told them the truth: that he was commanding a nuclear sub for a top-secret mission in the Baltic.

"Anyway, as you may have heard, they got this asinine father-son breakfast deal coming up. It's a helluva sham, but I'll tell you what, if you wanna get some free food out of it, I wouldn't mind."

"Mind, Coach?"

"Jesus, Rex. Head in the game, huh?" he said, tapping his forehead. "I wouldn't mind going to the breakfast. I wouldn't mind *accompanying* you to the breakfast. Not accompanying you, just sort of . . . we could both go. Together. Or separate. Just sort of sit at the same table and grab a couple of waffles on the school dime."

"Oh," I said. "Okay."

He looked up, squinting.

"Give it to me straight: You a waffle-man, Yancey?"

"I guess I could be."

"Good man."

I turned to leave.

"I mean, I don't want to make it a big deal or anything," he continued, still rocking in the chair. "Just if you want some waffles and I want some waffles, then why the hell shouldn't we be allowed some goddamned waffles, am I right? We pay taxes."

"Sure, Coach."

"And we live in a free, democratic society. Did you know that?"

I nodded.

"Good." He reached for a pen and pulled his half-finished maze close. "Well all right then. Get the hell out of here. I got some work to do."

✳   ✳   ✳

Housen was about as far from resembling my father as humanly possible. The man was a tower, one perfectly tuned, forty-year-old muscle. He had a large, doughy face and hands that could easily grip a football. Enormous feet, too, and a neck so thick his whistle turned into a choke collar. I'd never seen him wear anything but his world-famous sweatpants and collared shirt combo, but for our breakfast, he managed pants and a tie. A blazer, even, in place of the windbreaker. Complete with a clean shave, I almost didn't recognize him. He waited for me outside the cafeteria before school, running a plastic comb through his still-wet hair.

"Rex, two-time it," he hissed, shoving the comb back into his pocket. "You want those waffles or what?"

I dropped my backpack in the hall alongside the others and we took our place in the food line.

Daryl was there with his father, Mr. Harbeck, and after Coach and I loaded up on cantaloupe and waffles and blueberry muffins, we made the slow, treacherous walk over to their table without spilling.

"Greg Housen," Coach said, turning to Mr. Harbeck. "Glad to know ya." He stuck out his paw, then excused himself to "top off" his coffee.

Daryl leaned forward in his chair.

"So Housen's your dad, huh?"

I shrugged. I said there were probably worse fathers.

Near the end of the breakfast, Principal Cody made the mistake of asking if anyone wanted to say a few words. Coach Housen wasn't the only one to speak. Plenty of fathers did. They were all calm and self-assured, walking briskly to the microphone reeking of aftershave, checking their watches as they went.

Each speech started off with a joke like, "The thing about the father-son breakfast is . . ." and ended with something slightly sentimental about how proud they were to be fathers.

After four or five identical speeches ("So let's raise an orange juice to these boys . . ."), Coach Housen got around to loitering near enough to the podium to work his way into the line-up. When he finally settled in front of the microphone, he tapped it twice.

"This thing on?" His voice reverberated throughout the cafeteria.

He turned to the principal.

"Doesn't sound like it's on, Cody. You break it?"

The crowd of fathers assured him that it was, in fact, in working order, and after three or four "You sure's?" and "Testing one, two, three's" and "Give me a wave from the back if you can hear me," eventually he got around to believing them.

Coach cleared his throat and said, "All right, all right, settle down now."

The fathers did as they were told.

"Greg Housen, class of '76," he introduced himself. "Former varsity running back." The fathers nodded, as if they too were once inducted into the fraternity of middle school football. Coach leaned an elbow on the podium and continued.

"As you're all aware, I'm the head football coach here at Elmwood Middle, but here's something you probably didn't know: it's an honor and a privilege coaching your sons."

He paused, leaving room for the deafening cheers that did not come. A few clapped, a few returned their attention to their coffee.

"Now, I mean that," he said, pacing. "None of that blowing smoke up your ass bullwonky." Principal Cody bit his lip, directing his eyes to his cufflinks. "You see, you've got some good boys here with you today, and as a man without children, I've always felt a certain . . . kinship to your kids, sort of like an uncle figure."

A couple of fathers murmured in agreement.

"Regrettably," he continued, pointing to his crotch, "the good Lord did not see fit to bless me with strong swimmers. And it's a medical fact that I've got some cloggy pipes. Now, I could get into the science behind it, give you a brief lesson in sperm ducts, but I don't want Cody to piss himself in front of all you fine gentlemen who have joined us here today. Suffice it to say, I've always enjoyed being the uncle. But this morning, I'm more than an uncle to one player. Because this morning, I'm here to fill in for Rex Yancey's father – go ahead, Rex, raise your hand."

Did I have to?

"Come on, Rex. Don't be shy."

I raised it.

"Anywho," Coach continued, rapping his fingers against the podium, "I guess what I'm trying to say is, every young man needs an uncle. Also," he continued, listing them off on his fingers, "foot ball teams need players and equipment and water jugs and athletic tape and all of that, but that's neither here nor there. Because I'm here to talk about my son-for-the-day, Rex Yancey, and how the kid's a helluva kicker and you can all expect great things from him."

Was he talking hypothetically?

The fathers took their cue to clap. Mr. Harbeck patted my shoulder, gave me an undeserved thumbs up.

Housen's tear ducts seemed to be in working order, and while he tried hiding his emotions with his gigantic palm, we couldn't ignore the wails. He held up a finger with his opposite hand, then turned to face the wall. We watched his heaving shoulders as he wept, listened to his sea lion-like moans reverberate throughout the cafeteria.

"Shit, Housen," he ordered after a moment, "pull yourself to gether." He slapped his face a couple of times, rolled his shoulders.

Nobody knew what to do, especially not Principal Cody, who occupied the space between the podium and the wall. A few of my teammates started whispering.

"Hey Rex," Daryl mumbled, "do something about your dad, would you?"

"This interview is over," Housen said, his voice cracking as he left the podium.

By the time he meandered back to the table, I was already gone.

Those wind sprints really helped.

* * *

The first time I missed a field goal we were up by nine with six seconds left and it didn't really matter. But the second time – the second time Coach Housen overlooked first stringer Bryan Markum and told me to get my "sweet little heiny" in there, that he'd had a religious vision in which Jesus Christ and the Virgin Mary had assured him that I would "kick us to thy holy victory," – we were down by two (8–6) with about three minutes left. I hadn't even been paying much attention to the game. I'd heard a lot of shouting about Markum's making a couple of field goals, but ever since halftime, Daryl and I had devoted ourselves exclusively to putting Pop Rocks in our Gatorade and daring each other to drink it.

"How much you wanna bet your stomach will explode?"

"How much *you* wanna bet?"

"Yancey," Coach interrupted, "take us home, huh?"

Home? Was the game already over?

He snapped and pointed to the field.

"Get in there."

I looked out at all those grass-stained players with their hands on their hips and wondered what they wanted with me.

"Field goal, Yancey!" Couch explained. "Now move it!"

I couldn't figure out what I'd done with my helmet, so Daryl let me borrow his. It was too big. It made me look like a bobble head. I sort of bumbled past the rest of the team on the sidelines, excusing myself – "Sorry, pardon me, my bad, watch your feet there . . ." – as I hopped over their cleats.

I took the field – only the third time all season – and tried orienting myself with the goalpost.

Okay. The bleachers are there and the football is here, so according to the Transitive Property . . .

After finding my bearings, I huddled around my newfound team. Everything reeked of bad breath and crotches.

"So what'd I miss?" I asked them, wrapping my arms around the two people closest to me. They pushed me away.

"You gonna make this or what?" asked linebacker Trent Gordon, a beefy kid who looked like the aftermath of a failed attempt at the world's first human-bull hybrid.

"Sure," I nodded.

Why not?

Then, we broke from the huddle, and I made up some elaborate equation involving wind direction and ball speed and the velocity and degree to which my foot would most likely come in contact with its target.

I took five steps backward, two to the left, just like Bryan Markum had taught me.

As the official stuck the whistle in his mouth the other team called a time out.

"Oh for crying out loud," Coach hollered, his hands above his head. "Yancey, run that sweet ass over here for me!"

I ran it over.

"Now look," he said, a hand clasped to my buttocks. "They're just trying to freeze you up. That's all this is. Look at 'em all huddled up over there. Just a bunch of little ladies. They're not saying a goddamned thing. You know why they called a time out? Freeze you up. Get you nervous. Get those butterflies really pumping in your stomach." He began spanking me to the rhythm of his words. "But don't – *smack* – get – *smack* – nervous."

Smack, smack.

Coach's hand on my ass had proved quite distracting, and between all the smacking all I'd heard was: "freeze you up," "get you nervous," "butterflies in stomach."

"So what are you waiting for?" he asked, bestowing me with one final spanking. "Get in there and do it." He sort of chased after me to try to squeeze in one last ass-slap, but once more, the wind sprints served a purpose.

I took five steps backward, two to the left.

The official blew his whistle.

I kicked.

The crowd roared.

And as the stadium lights highlighted every fleck of sweat, every tensed muscle, every held breath, the football trickled somewhere in the high weeds near the fence.

My father called home on a Tuesday. I remember.

"Rexy!" he cried. "How's it hanging? How's football?"

"Okay," I said. "How's . . . painting?"

"Eh, not so good, really. Turns out it wasn't painting I needed. I thought I needed painting, but you know what I really had a hankering for?"

"What?"

"A sports car! Who knew, right?"

"You bought a sports car?"

"Mmmhmm," he said proudly. "Mazda Miata. The poor man's Ferrari. You're gonna love it, Rexy. Trust me. The salesman called it an orgasm on wheels. You know what that means, right?"

"Oh," I said. "That sounds . . . neat."

"Hey, is your mom there? Can you put her on for me?"

I handed it over to Mom. She was smiling so wide I thought her face might break. In fact, maybe it did because she was crying.

"A what on wheels?" she blushed. "Honey! Please!" she said, lowering her voice, "Rex's standing right here."

Dad mumbled something else.

"Really?" she asked, brightening. "Yes, well, I'm sure I will, too."

She nodded, smiling, tears streaking down her face, smearing her make-up.

"Well when can we expect you . . . Uh-huh . . . Sure! No, that's perfect . . . I know he's really missed you, too . . . Yes, a lot to talk about . . . Yes . . . but it's over? For good?"

I wandered into the living room where I didn't have to listen.

"Okay," Mom agreed. "Well, we can't wait, either . . . Back to normal sounds fine."

I tossed the telephone books into a trash bag and then walked it out to the curb. The garbage trucks wouldn't arrive for another two days, but at least I could count on them to be there.

❋ ❋ ❋

After several unsuccessful attempts, I finally proved Coach Housen, Jesus Christ, and the Virgin Mary right: I sailed a ball squarely through the goalposts. It didn't matter. We were down by forty-two.

Our team dinner was held two weeks later, at a pizza place where the servers wore red and white checkered hats and spoke with fake Italian accents.

"Mama mia!" they cried every time you ordered. "Wouldja like-a side-a breadsticks with the nacho cheese?"

All our parents were there, and Coach Housen seemed a little overwhelmed by the nearly two to one adult to adolescent ratio. Our parents were busy chitchatting about things unrelated to football. That same day, our English teacher, Ms. Steinberg, had assigned us a book with the word "cock" in it, and Adam Green's mother had made it her personal mission to get the book pulled from the curriculum. She was passing around a petition, asking people to please refrain from spilling marinara on it.

Dad was there, his arm around Mom, and all I heard him say was, "Cock, cock, cock. I guess I just don't see what the big deal is."

After that, everyone thought he was just about the world's greatest dad; they didn't even know about his mug, or his vanishing act, or the video game he brought me upon his return. When one of the fathers asked why he hadn't been at the games, Dad mentioned something about a "soul-sucking business trip." He didn't mention anything about impressionist painting; he'd simply slipped back into our lives like a turpentine-soaked paintbrush.

Housen stared at the menu for twenty minutes or so, occasionally jotting a note on the kid's menu with a blue crayon.

"Ready to order?" the waitress asked for about the hundredth time. She'd long since dropped the accent.

Housen sighed. His eyes caught mine.

"Just order some pepperonis," I coached. "Everyone likes pepperoni."

He nodded, closing the menu.

"We'll do that. We'll take a coupla pepperonis," he told her. "And a coupla those meat lovers, too."

Housen handed her the menu before excusing himself to the bathroom. Ten minutes passed, and since I wasn't sure if he was ever coming back, I slunk in after him.

I found him there, leaning against the sink, practicing his end-of-the-year-speech in the mirror.

He stopped when I entered.

"Rexy, hey there," he said, glancing at me through the reflection. He folded his speech and returned it to his pocket. "Pizza here yet?"

"Not yet," I said. He cleared his throat. His face had whitened, sweat stains permeating his collared shirt.

"Just rehearsing," he explained. "Want to make sure I tell your parents how you all went out there and really nabbed 'em by their dongers this year," he chuckled, slapping my shoulder. "Dincha?"

I hesitated.

"You know, Coach. Sometimes people think that the things you say . . . well, that they sound sort of gay."

"Gay?" he laughed. "What could possibly be gay about football?" I didn't mention the guy-on-guy dog piles or the naked showers that followed.

"Well, like when you tell us to 'whip their dicks' sometimes. 'Nab their dongers' would be another example, I guess."

He pulled the blue crayon from his pocket and began revising his speech.

"You goddamned kids. Ten years ago no one would've bat an eye. Now, I can't even say 'dongers' without the PC police riding my asshole . . ."

"Not that you have to go and change everything," I explained. "Just maybe be careful about what you say. Especially because Adam's mom is kind of a nut and . . . well, you know her. She'll probably make everyone sign a petition or something. Against gay people."

Coach's nose flared. He snapped the crayon in his hand.

"Gay," he repeated, shaking his head and staring into the sink. "Suddenly I'm gay because I'm molding you boys into hard men."

"Hard, Coach?"

"Oh, let me guess: that's gay, too, right?"

"I wouldn't call it . . ."

"Am I some kind of . . . gay because I want you to have a winning season? Cuz I want to teach you a few fundamentals about the game?"

"Coach, maybe I didn't say it right. All I was trying to say was . . ."

He grabbed me by my shirt collar and pulled me into the parking lot.

"Wind sprints," he shouted. "Count 'em off, Yancey."

I stared out at the half-filled lot. A family excused themselves and walked past us.

"Well? What are you waiting for? Count 'em off!"

"Coach, maybe later, okay?"

I started to brush past him but he stopped me. He put his trembling hands on my arms and held me there.

"Come on, Coach. They're waiting for us."

He breathed heavily, then let his hands drop to his sides.

"We're a team, Yancey," he said, his eyes closed. "Remember back when we were a team?"

I snuck past him, taking a seat beside my father.

Housen had a box of trophies and, thankfully, didn't award me any of them. I was already "sucking Housen's ball sac," according to Trent Gordon. But not anymore.

Adam Green took Most Valuable Player and a tight-end named Richard Vix unsurprisingly took Most Improved.

"Hey, they don't call him tight-end for nothing," Housen chuckled when Richard rose to collect his trophy. He caught himself too late, but nobody thought anything of it but me.

Then, Housen started in on his speech, omitting most of the parts about crotches and groins and tight heineys. It made for a pretty short presentation. He just elaborated on how we should be proud of our 8–6 record, how it was a team effort built on grit and dedication, and how there was no "win" in "team."

"Cuz when you rearrange the letters," he clarified, "it doesn't spell win. I guess you could spell 'meat' or 'tame' or 'meta,' but you can't spell 'win.' Not with those letters."

The parents nodded.

"But the real turning point in our season," he continued, "had to be when ol' Rex Yancey sailed that perfect field goal right between the crossbars. Remember that kick? Against Davenport? The kid's got a leg on him, am I right? Anyway, thank you very much."

Housen sat down and sipped his lemon water. A few of the parents clapped. Dad tousled my hair, then turned to the rest of the parents and said, "I gave 'em that leg, you know."

After dinner, everyone dawdled in the parking lot while Mrs. Green tried to fill out the snack assignments for the upcoming basketball season.

"You trying out for basketball?" Dad asked. Daryl and the others were busy playing monkey-in-the-middle with the Most Improved trophy.

"Naw," I said, watching them. "I don't think so."

"Why the hell not?"

"I don't know. The coach sort of sucks. He makes everyone run till they puke."

"Builds character," Dad pointed out. "Puking always builds character."

We leaned against Dad's Miata while Mom continued chatting up the mothers.

"How's she been?" Dad asked, fiddling with his toothpick as he watched her gesturing to the others.

"She's been okay."

He nodded.

"I didn't slip off because of her. She knows that."

"Okay."

"Not because of you either," he added. "I just . . . I got this itch. Sometimes you just gotta scratch it, know what I'm saying?"

I didn't.

Eventually, the three of us rendezvoused, scrunching ourselves into the tiny car. Mom sat on my lap.

"Buckled in?" Dad asked.

"Buckled!" Mom smiled. She was trying hard to love him more than ever.

Nearby, Coach Housen carried the empty trophy box to his Blazer, blocking the center lane of the lot.

"Move it or lose it, pal!" Dad honked, revving his engine. He didn't even recognize him.

I slouched low in my seat as we screeched past, hiding behind my mother. In the rearview, I saw Coach remove his hat and clasp his hands before him.

Dad shouted so we could hear him over the wind.

"She's pretty nice with the top down, isn't she?"

✳ ✳ ✳

A year later Dad drove off for an oil change, only he never came back. His paintbrushes and easel were still in the garage so we didn't bother calling Vermont. In fact, we didn't call anyone. He was no longer worth the long distance.

I graduated from the eighth grade later that year, and at the closing exercises Principal Cody called my name for the Faculty Prize, an award sort of like a sportsmanship award for academics, to the guy who got a lot of Cs but seemed to work pretty hard for them. Later that night, we had punch and cookies by the tetherball courts behind the school.

We were having a good time when I noticed Housen far off near the baseball field, chalking the lines with the roller.

I wandered over, watching him from behind the aluminum bleachers.

Housen started work on the third baseline, then wiped his brow and leaned against the backstop.

He turned, spotting me.

"Well look who it is! Mr. Rex Yancey in the flesh!"

I came out from hiding.

"Heard you took Faculty Prize. I told 'em you were a hard worker. Christ, I'd been saying it for years."

"Thanks, Coach."

He shrugged, spitting into the dirt, then rubbing it in with his shoe.

He continued chalking. I followed a few steps behind.

"Ever seen one of these?" he asked, pointing to the roller.

"I've seen them."

"You ever use one?"

I shook my head.

"Here."

He handed it off to me.

"Now the trick is to get the lines nice and straight. Just keep your eye on the base ahead of you. That's the trick. If you look straight down at the chalk your line will be all cockeyed." He rephrased: "It won't look . . . good."

I nodded, working the roller up and down the dust.

"There you go," he coached. "Nice and easy, give her a generous dusting."

Far off, by the tetherballs, fathers were gathering their sons beneath their arms, telling jokes, smiling.

"Got any summer plans?" he asked me, breaking my stare.

"Oh, I don't know," I shrugged. "I'll probably mow some lawns. Try to save some money. For college or something. I should start early."

He nodded.

"Well there's always a football scholarship. I wouldn't rule that out entirely."

"Naw, I really should just mow, probably."

He laughed, patting my shoulder. "There you go again, always doing things the hard way, aren't ya?"

I nodded.

He looked at me as if trying to solve a riddle.

"All right, give me that," he said at last, commandeering the chalk roller. "I'll take 'er from here. Get the hell out of here. Go enjoy your summer. Be a kid. Raise some hell."

"I'll try."

"You better do more than try!" he laughed. "Mothers lock up your daughters, you know what I mean?" he winked.

I nodded.

"Get on, then," he shooed, waving me off, and continued chalking the lines.

But I didn't.

I just planted myself on the bleachers, waiting.

Around town, people were turning on bug zappers and lighting citronella candles and extending hammocks between the lengths of trees. They were waiting in line for ice-cream cones or filling out job applications or shooting baskets in somebody's drive. They were sliding into backyard pools and riding skateboards. Pyramiding the charcoal on the bottoms of grills and adjusting the sprinkler heads. Walking barefoot. Drinking orange sodas. Dodging the low swooping bats.

Meanwhile, I just sat on those bleachers. And I'd sit there for another half an hour or so, until he finally exited the shed and noticed me there.

I don't remember much after that. It was all so long ago.

Probably, we just wandered, kicking up dust and trying not to disturb the freshly laid chalk.

Just talked. Talked and talked.

Until there were no words left for us to say, nowhere left for us to wander.

Dixie Land

In his mind, The Confederate lived in a log cabin in the backwaters of Tennessee, beside a rocky canyon and a stream that, many years back, overflowed with the thick blood of Yankees.

Though in reality, he resided in a twentieth-century Cape Cod on the outskirts of Nashville. A glowing BP sign illuminated just beyond the neighborhood trees. It was a fine home, complete with a two-car garage, a professionally manicured lawn, even a WELCOME mat in the backyard that played "Dixie" when stepped upon with the necessary force.

The Confederate had a son, Confederate Junior, though most called him Junior for short. Still clinging to his baby fat, the fresh-faced seven-year-old was thick around the midsection, though what he lacked in physical prowess he more than made up for with gusto.

While training in the backyard, The Confederate often commanded, "Junior! Bayonet ready?" to which his son snapped to attention, proclaiming, "Yes sir, Drill Sergeant, sir!"

It was a declaration that caused the old man's heart to swell.

His son – *his own flesh and blood* – possessed the ability to maim and wound and return honor to the Confederate States of America.

"Then affix bayonet, dear child!"

Junior attached the metal blade to the end of a rifle with the diligence of a well-trained soldier under the command of General Thomas Jonathan Stonewall Jackson – God rest his soul and bless him. It was all one glorious motion: the insertion of the blade, the quarter turn, followed by a stomped foot.

The Confederate cared deeply for his son, proving it each time they went hunting in the woods. When their stalking ended in gunfire, it was Junior's shot that broke the soundless forest first. The Confederate resisted his itchy finger, only indulging in the safety shot after his son's barrel was already cleared. Junior – still young and not yet calloused by war – often missed, and it was The Confederate's shot that typically downed the deer, its knobby legs crumpling to the vegetation first while the remainder of heft toppled soon after.

After each kill, Junior asked innocently, "Affix bayonet?"

And while his father fully appreciated the gusto with which his son slaughtered, he had to deny the request.

"Sorry, pal," he'd say, clapping a hand to his son's grays. "Think this one's already dead."

❋ ❋ ❋

The Confederate had a wife, a maker of time machines. She was a stay-at-home-scientist whose paychecks were stamped with the insignia of Vanderbilt University, though her work received private funding from blackout groups within the deepest bowels of the U.S. government. Once a failed psychic, she had turned her attention to the tangibles, the ease of atomic weights, the certainty of conductors. If she wanted to see the future, she reasoned, then she would have to build it herself. Two PhD's later (one in rocket science, CalTech Class of '94; the other quantum mechanics, MIT '01) she walked across a stage, shook a few hands (endured a few jokes about being called "Dr. Dr."), and earned herself a glimpse into the unknown.

When asked what she did for a living, The Confederate boiled it down more simply: "She's a Yankee sympathizer!" It wasn't entirely true, though he thought it accurate enough.

He had convinced himself that his wife's interest in overcoming the barriers of the time-space continuum would inevitably benefit the North.

"But Charlie, don't you see?" his wife argued. "The benefits of time travel would positively impact all of us. The *entire* country. It would allow us the privilege of foresight."

"Oh, Lynda," he chuckled, shaking his head. "That's all well and good, but you've forgotten about *hindsight*, dear. Does anyone ever stop to consider hindsight? The lessons of the past?"

In the early years of their marriage, he'd obsessed over her work, causing her to wonder if that's where the attraction lay. He could often be found loitering in the basement, casually inquiring what that button did, or that wire. Faithfully, she would explain everything, adding the occasional, "But please, don't touch. I mean it."

He'd pause, his hands hovering just inches over the machinery, the bulbs and switches beckoning for him to come just a little bit closer. He'd absorb all he could, even when he only understood half of it.

"So let me get this straight," he reasoned, clearing his throat. "Time travel goes both ways, right? I mean, let's say I want to go to the Battle of Fredericksburg, but later, I wanted to jump to . . . I don't know, the Battle of Vicksburg. Then on to some future battle that hasn't even happened yet. Something with lasers. Lasers versus Robots. Could I do that? Could I go to the Lasers versus Robots war directly from the Battle of Antietam? From a scientific perspective, I mean. What's your expert opinion?"

"Well . . . technically," his wife conceded, erasing the formulas and speaking only in hypotheticals. "That's our great hope; that we might correct the errors of the past while simultaneously testing the future. But it's more complicated than that. There are paradoxes to consider, causality, mutable timelines. I think you're failing to see the drastic ramifications of altering the cosmic plan . . ."

"Uh-huh," he agreed, stroking his beard. "Cosmic plan. You hit the nail on the head with that one, hon. But let's say I have a hankering to pay a little visit to John Brown at Harper's Ferry, but first, maybe I want to swing by Fort Wayne and pick up George Washington's sword . . ."

Logic was not his strong suit, though much like his son, his shortcomings were minor in comparison to his determination.

Once, many years back, under cover of darkness, he'd snuck into Chattanooga Military Park and set to work removing a plaque proclaiming the site a "Union victory" – an assessment The Confederate deemed highly suspect, little more than another example of Northern revisionist history. A park ranger discovered him mid-removal and removed him instead, hauling The Confederate to the county jail on two separate charges: trespassing and defacing public property.

"The crime here," The Confederate spat while being guided into the backseat of the squad car, "is you thinking I've done something wrong. *I'm* setting the record straight. And now you've gone and made me a prisoner of war . . . there's really no telling how the Rebels will respond . . ."

"There's no war," the park ranger sighed wearily. "Just because you're wearing the uniform doesn't mean there's a war."

After receiving a written warning and a light slap on the wrist, he was released the following morning, all charges dropped, provided he never again set foot in the park.

"I promise," he saluted. "Scout's honor."

Yet by the following evening, his steadfast determination overpowered any notions of honor. He returned to the park, completing his mission without further interruption, all while humming the tune of "Dixie."

At midnight, from atop a silent bluff, he hurled the plaque into the mighty Chattanooga, the rushing water washing away what it couldn't erase completely.

✳   ✳   ✳

The Confederate never considered himself a "Civil War eccentric," one of those "live-in-the-past" kind of guys. After all, his home contained all the necessary accouterments.

Running water in every sink.

Electricity.

They even had a computer with Internet access, though The Confederate found this particular luxury excessive ("Tell me one thing the Internet's got that you can't find in the *Farmer's Almanac*").

Yet despite technology's intrusion, theirs was a happy home. In the evenings, when he returned from his job as a grounds crewman at the local high school, he was often greeted by his son's attempts at recreating historically accurate representations of key Civil War battles along their living room floor. Junior strategically arranged his plastic green soldiers along the ridgeline of the couch, continually revising their formations.

But upon returning home one August afternoon – hands still reverberating from the shakes of the mower, shoelaces dyed green – he was surprised to find Junior positioning his men along the dinner table instead. Far below, the Yankees were scattered mercilessly on the carpet.

"If that's supposed to be the Battle of Ball's Bluff, then your scale's all wrong," The Confederate warned. "How many feet to an inch, do you figure?" He squatted beside his son, eyeballing it. "I'd give it about five feet per inch. Sound about right?"

"Huh?" Junior asked, noticing his father's presence for the first time.

"Ball's Bluff," The Confederate repeated. "You know."

"What about it?"

"That's the battle you got going here, right?" he asked, fiddling with the men. "You got your Confederates here, driving the Yankees over the bluff right here, and this down here's the Potomac. Made good use of the flank, I see, and the frontal attack. Just your scale's off, that's all. Nothing we can't fix."

Junior shook his head.

"It's not Ball's Bluff."

"Bean Station?"

"No."

"Well, sheesh, Junior. If this is some sorry excuse for Mossy Creek, then I've got to say, you've done a pretty shoddy job handling the counterattack. Just have a look at . . ."

"Dad, this is a battle you don't know yet."

The Confederate clamped the insides of his cheeks, trying to keep from laughing.

"Oh, a battle I don't know yet," he smiled. "Well, by all means, enlighten me."

"Well, for one thing, it's a battle from the future," Junior confided, still fiddling with his men.

"Says who?"

"Says Mom. She saw it. When she went there."

The Confederate's smug smile dissipated. He pushed on his knees and rose, tearing toward the bedroom.

"Lynda!"

"She's sleeping. She's tired now. From all that traveling."

"Lynda," he called even louder. "You in here? You in here, love?" He swung the bedroom door wide, spying her pale, bare feet on the carpet beside the bed.

"Lynda!" he said, running to her.

She stared up at him with empty eyes. Sweat dampened the top of her blouse. Her legs were exposed above the knee. An array of different colored sensors remained suction-cupped to her forehead, their wires snaking to a small, metallic shoebox. All switches were set to off, all knobs returned to zero. She shuddered as he plucked the sensors off of her and placed a hand to her forehead.

"You're freezing," he whispered. "Jesus, why are you freezing?"

She gasped, trying to allow the words to croak from her throat.

"I've seen the future," she whispered, her eyelids fluttering.

"And?"

She squeezed both hands tight on his wrist.

"It is not . . . good."

While The Confederate preferred his own version of time travel (fewer wormholes, more fire pits), he nonetheless recognized the value of his wife's own contributions.

And so, when time allowed, he left her to her work and set out on afternoon noodling expeditions in the open waters of the Cumberland River. He was well practiced, and after years of refinement, had become quite the proficient noodler – perhaps the finest in the tri-county region. It required little skill: simply mustering the courage to dangle an arm into the freezing river and waiting for something to bite. Typically, the "something" was a catfish of impossible size, its whiskers miniature whips, its razor-sharp teeth two dozen reminders why one should never attempt to go noodling. Still, it was an enjoyable enough pastime – an activity that reminded him of his own childhood – and a tradition he looked forward to passing on to his son.

"So . . . what do we do exactly?" Junior asked. They tromped through the wilderness in coonskin caps and deer-hide pants. This, The Confederate confided, was to help maintain a certain level of authenticity.

"Well, the first thing you gotta do is block your mind of fear."

"Okay," Junior nodded, blinking twice. "Then what?"

"You're already done blocking your mind of fear?"

"Uh-huh. I did it awhile ago."

"Well, okay then," The Confederate smiled proudly. "Thatta boy. So next you'll want to hunt for a good part of the river, some place that doesn't flow too quickly."

They found just the place – a narrowing brook sequestered between a rocky embankment and a few downed limbs. Father and son – careful not to let the tails of their coonskin caps fall into the water – lay belly down and stared hard into the stream.

"Now you want to get yourself mentally prepared. And it's not as easy as it looks. But once you are . . ."

The Confederate took a few seconds to close his eyes and breathe deep. His heavy exhales caused his beard to waver.

"But once you are," he repeated, "you dunk your arm in, all the way up to the shoulder, you see." He demonstrated, the cold creeping through him, the low, slow ache pulsing from fingertip to elbow.

"Then what?"

"Well, then you wait."

A moment passed, and the cold water entered his bones. The Confederate gritted teeth, trying to block it out. He envisioned a sunny battlefield in the summer of 1864, men playing cards, smoking cigars, far, far away from the water.

Junior looked hard at the ground, staring at an anthill.

"How you feeling, kid?" The Confederate chattered. "Brave?"

"Pretty brave, I guess."

"Okay, then you'll want to go ahead and put your arm in beside mine. Don't worry, you'll adjust to the temperature."

Junior considered it, eventually closing his eyes and imitating his father's heavy breathing. The breaths continued, growing noisily, and finally, after much fanfare, Junior opened his eyes once more and said, "Couldn't I just affix bayonet instead?"

"No, sir," The Confederate chuckled. "Not for noodling. No bayonets required."

Junior paused. He peered down.

"So what's down there anyway? Like, fish?"

"Well, sure, some fish, I'd imagine."

"How about snakes?"

"Sure. That's possible."

Junior paused once more before continuing.

"Are there skeletons down there, do you think?"

The Confederate smiled.

"Well sure, pal, probably a few Yanks. But they're not gonna bother you. We got 'em a long time ago, remember?" The Confederate winked. "You can thank your forefathers for that."

Junior moved toward the river, his shaky hand tapping the top layer of water, his skin sticking from the wetness. He inched deeper, his entire arm suddenly plunging into the heart of the river, gripping it as it gripped him.

"Good!" The Confederate cried. "That's the spirit! Just like that."

Junior trembled, wincing and keeping his eyes closed tight. The Confederate heard a low humming escape from somewhere within his son's chest. A war cry, perhaps. Or a whimper.

"Hey, come on now. Time to be a man," The Confederate said. "Besides, if these fish have any sense in 'em, they'll go for the bigger bait."

"Are you sure?"

"'Course I'm sure! I'm your father."

The Confederate listened to his son's whimpers.

Then, he bulged his bicep, made himself the bigger bait.

❋　❋　❋

On the days Lynda required peace and quiet for her work, The Confederate and his son practiced drill commands in the yard. The house freshly silent, she retreated once more to the shallows of the mildewed basement, reexamining the structural integrity of her time dilator, her photon reader, seeking out a better future.

Meanwhile, father and son fit themselves into a past of their own making, pulling on britches and wielding guns. Powerful guns. The kind that didn't allow for mistakes.

They marched, their rifles tucked tight alongside shoulders, their chests thrust out like peacocks.

"Present, arms!"

Junior attempted a rifle salute until his father allowed him to stop.

"Order, arms!"

They marched a bit more, boots clomping in the flower garden, displacing the mulch and the bulbs while the neighbors watched on from their windows.

"About, face!"

Junior turned one hundred and eighty degrees, erect and silent.

"Forward, march!"

The Confederate smiled as his son responded to each and every command. He knew he could continue the orders for the remainder of the morning without complaint, that his son was a good and loyal soldier.

Much to his father's surprise, Junior's small frame managed the weight of the gun quite nicely. His childish chest carved hollows along the ridge of his stomach each time he inhaled, the gun fitting neatly in the space.

After drill, the pair collapsed beneath an oak in the backyard, sipping orange Gatorade, cooling their bodies and restoring their electrolytes in the swelter of the shade. The Confederate had a stick in his left hand and busied himself drawing schematics in the dirt for the benefit of his son. Junior nodded attentively, though he'd heard them all before. There were only so many battles worth remembering.

"So what that ol' rascal Beauregard did was, he moved his troops *north* of Shiloh, like this," The Confederate explained, drawing various x's into the dirt. "You see, what Beauregard knew that Grant didn't was that the terrain was highly vulnerable to sneak attacks. And he exploited that knowledge. Old Beauregard pushed the Yanks all the way back to the Tennessee River, right here, when all of the sudden . . ."

"We won."

"Jesus, kid, I'm trying to tell you the story."

"But we did win, right? Because of Beauregard's fine leadership and the cowardice of the Union army? That's what you told me, isn't it?"

"Well, that's how it *should've* happened. Most historians chalked it up as a loss for the good guys, but most of those historians are piss poor Northerners anyway so you kind of have to take what they say with a grain of . . ."

"Dad," Junior squinted, picking dirt from beneath his nails. "Did we really win *any* of those battles?"

"Well, sure! Ever hear of a little something called The Battle of Chickamauga? Fort Pillow? Paducah and Petersburg? And then you got your Battle of Poison Spring, of course . . ."

"So why didn't we win the war?"

"Christ, don't they teach you anything in school?"

He shrugged.

The Confederate brushed the dirt from his pants and began pacing.

"It's like this," he sighed, motioning with his hands. "The winners and losers all depend on who the hell's telling the story. Make sense?"

Shrugging, Junior stood, then moved toward the kitchen to refill his glass with Gatorade. Along the way, his foot clipped the WELCOME mat and "Dixie" began humming throughout the yard.

"And just wait till your mother wraps up work on her time machine," The Confederate called after him. "Then we'll see who won."

* * *

As the summer wound down – after their talk beneath the shady oak – The Confederate found his son's zeal for southern independence beginning to wane.

"Want to drill?" he'd ask, and by mid-September, Junior's shrugs had turned into no's.

"Well why the hell not?"

"Homework," he'd explain. "Ms. Henson's sort of a bear about it."

The Confederate tried hard not to take the rebuffs personally. Homework was important, after all. Occasionally, he'd catch Lynda nodding at Junior's response, as if approving his responsible decision.

"You don't have to encourage him, you know," he told her one night in bed.

"Encourage him to do what?"

"Not to drill with me."

Lynda's eyes were closed, her hands on the cool side of the pillow.

"Honey, I just think that maybe your... reverence for the past hasn't quite rubbed him the same way."

"Sometimes I don't think it's rubbed him at all."

"Why do you think that is?"

"Cuz he figures we're a bunch of stuffy-britches-wearing losers."

"Why would he think that?"

"Well, because the britches are stuffy, for one. Plus, he thinks all we ever do is lose battles."

"Well, the Confederacy did lose quite a few..."

"*We*," he pressed, rocking her shoulder, "*we* lost quite a few, Lynda."

"*I* didn't lose anything."

The Confederate changed the subject.

"Anything new with the time machine?"

"A bit."

"Anything I'd understand?"

She shrugged.

"That's okay," he nodded, tucking himself beneath the covers and flicking off the light. "Just don't forget to carry the one, huh?"

He kissed her cheek, and they turned quiet together.

A moment later, he broke the silence.

"But it's going to work, right?" he asked. "I mean, one of these days."

"Sure, Charlie, one of these days."

"And it's going to show us a bright future?"

She paused, turning to face the window.

"If I can get there first."

That night, The Confederate dreamed of bugles and drum lines and an entire cavalry of sneering, dust-clouded warhorses. The men atop them were painted gray, swords drawn, glistening. One of them, a ghost soldier, cantered away from the others, pulling his reins just inches from The Confederate's dreaming face.

"What . . . what do you want?" The Confederate mumbled in his sleep.

The ghost soldier cleared his throat and then, quite robustly, broke into song:

O, I wish I was in Dixie!
Hooray! Hooray!
In Dixie Land I'll take my stand,
To Live and Die in Dixie!

He saluted – trotting off into somebody else's dream – and in the morning, when The Confederate woke, he found himself humming the tune.

✳ ✳ ✳

After breakfast, father and son went into the woods just like father and son. There were no Confederates – no army grays or C.S.A. buckles or anything.

"It's kind of nice," Junior admitted, revisiting a familiar complaint, "not having to wear those stuffy, old uniforms. It's a lot cooler without the britches."

The Confederate stayed silent, staring down at his chicken legs lost in his rarely worn cargo shorts.

All around them, the woods were alive with animals. Already, they'd spotted two white-tailed deer and a fox, and each time, instinctually, The Confederate lifted his arms as if attempting to fire a gun he wasn't holding.

"Affix bayonet?" Junior joked, and they shared a good laugh from the old days.

That morning, they viewed nature in a different way – something to treasure, something worth preserving. They even paid notice to the mockingbirds and irises that followed them along their path. The Confederate identified all that he could – coralberry, bluebells, Virginia willows – and much to his surprise, Junior seemed enraptured by his knowledge.

"So can you just plant them anywhere?" he asked of the wood sunflower, to which his father replied, "Well, they tend to flourish best in damp climates. Need a helluva lot of rain and sun to make it much past August . . ."

In the dead of September, most of the flowers had already sunk their heavy heads. But The Confederate and Junior paid closest attention to the few that remained, brushing their fingertips atop the petals as if renewing them with life.

"Noodling?" Junior suggested upon reaching the river. The Confederate was only too happy to oblige.

Several weeks had passed since their last attempt, and while Junior had yet to receive so much as a nibble, The Confederate had felt the sinking teeth dig into his flesh on more than a few occasions.

The Confederate lay belly down along the bank and rolled up his sleeve.

"Shall we?"

Junior smiled, matching his father's motions.

They lay there, their backs warming in sunlight, the trees gathering shadows and cooling them in the dark, dappled patches of skin.

As they noodled, they discussed Ms. Henson's insistence on weekly vocabulary tests, how she deemed reading, writing, and mathematics far more important than social studies.

"But social studies is the key to everything!" The Confederate argued. "Jesus Christ! Who in their right mind would choose, actually *choose*, to gloss over the events that made our country what it is today? Take the War of Northern Aggression, for instance . . ."

"I know! That's what I told her!" Junior argued, "But she said . . ."

In mid-sentence, the fish rose up and latched onto Junior's arm. Junior screamed, helpless, as the gigantic golden-flecked beast dragged the boy into the river, down the river, and within moments, beneath the river, too.

"Son!" The Confederate called, jumping to his feet. "Junior!"

He dove into the cool current, eyes wide.

But ten minutes later, his frantic searching yielded little: driftwood, a rusted bobber, some tangled fishing line. And twenty minutes later, when he discovered his son's weed-wrapped body clinging to the shore – bite marks beyond the elbow – the search abruptly ended. Junior's t-shirt ballooned the way his lungs wouldn't, his shorts stuck tight to his knees.

The Confederate called for help. Only his echo called back.

* * *

They buried what they couldn't bring back. Buried him deep, in a coffin, in the ground, in the cemetery.

To the outside world, their grief appeared surprisingly short-lived: the result of propelling themselves headlong into their respective professional lives. Lynda's time travel productivity increased two-fold, and when The Confederate woke in the morning, he found the bed empty and cooling beside him. And at the end of the day, after brushing his teeth and returning once more to the bed, still, her space retained the empty shape she left him.

Almost nightly, he heard her clomping up the stairs – sometimes in the purple dawn of the morning – her face red, her hair clumped and matted.

Her hands were often stained chalk white from calculations, and when he asked about her findings, she'd pinch the top of her nose and close her eyes tight and say she had a terrible headache.

"What smells like burning?" he once asked and was surprised by her reply.

"My mind is."

Some nights they slept, some nights they didn't, but each morning he'd wake to find her missing. And twenty minutes later, after coffee and toast and a goodbye shout into the basement, he too returned to work. All day long, The Confederate damned the present and prayed for the past, but always, he kept his grief silent. There was simply no time for it.

After all, there were always dying flowers to unearth, always weeds in need of uprooting.

❋　❋　❋

The recurring dreams were too much for him. Too many gray horsemen. Too many bridles. Too many metal bits worked between the teeth of the horses' uncooperative mouths.

Always, he'd wake humming the same damn song, until eventually, even sleep became a luxury he could no longer seem to afford.

So instead of sleep, he drilled.

He drilled in the backyard in the nighttime. Drilled by the riverbed. Drilled by the trees. He drilled, kicking his feet and snapping his shoulders back, his movements amplified in shadow. Some nights, when he was brash and sleep-deprived, he stopped drilling long enough to plunge his arm into the icy heart of the river. Revenge was a word he understood and a concept he fully embraced. While the golden-flecked fish never returned – never dared a larger meal – it didn't stop The Confederate from trying.

"Come on, Yankee scum," he baited, "why doncha give this arm a try?"

The Confederate, a good soldier himself, remained steadfast and determined. And when the river offered nothing, he had no choice but to return once more to the yard, to the oak that had long since stopped growing, to the grass in need of a cut.

When he drilled, he drilled only in his finest confederate attire – his brass buttoned grays, dark britches, the cast iron belt buckle with the C.S.A. insignia. A sword dangled from his left hip, and he carried a rusted rifle.

"Slow march," he huffed to himself. "Slow march." And then, when he quickened his pace: "Quick march, soldier, quick march!"

The sweat, even in the cool dew of midnight, drizzled down his forehead. He shuddered from the cold, from the heat, and, as he continued his drills night after night, he began to notice the way the trees lost their leaves only in the darkest hours when he alone bore witness.

"To the front!" he demanded.

"Change step!"

"About face!"

The gun felt light in his hand, and the sword, weightless.

One night in mid-October, when Lynda saw him there, marching in moonlight, she stayed quiet. From the screen door, she watched as he ordered, "Mark time! Mark time!" again and again, his knees kicking up from the ground.

"Mark time! Mark time! Mark time, goddamn you!"

"Charlie," she whispered, slipping out the screen door. "Honey, I think time is marked." Oblivious, she stepped on the WELCOME mat, restarting the tune from his dream.

She leapt forward, but the song repeated, electronic music blips drifting from the mat.

"Honey..." she repeated, moving toward him.

"Mark time! Mark time! Soldier, mark time!" he called, overpowering "Dixie," searching once more for his gait beyond the music.

"Darling..."

"Mark time! About face! Mark time!"

"Shhh... just stop, soldier. Just halt. Please."

The WELCOME mat turned quiet and so did he.

She put her hands to his grays and said, "It's time for you to just stop now."

He peered into the woods.

"You know," she began, picking the lint from his jacket, "you look pretty heroic in uniform."

He didn't say anything.

"Are you cold?"

He shook his head no.

"Want me to top off the canteen?"

He held up a finger, then tilted his ear to the wind.

"You hear that? The Yankees are coming."

"No, they're all gone now. You know that."

He dropped his hand to his side, turned to her.

"How's your work? Are we there yet?"

"Getting there."

"Well, march quick, soldier," he begged. "Please march quicker."

"I'm trying, Charlie."

He reached for his canteen and drew deep from the metal container, wiping his face with his forearm.

"How long, you think, till it's finished?"

She stared at him, his hands quivering against his sword.

She could not give him the answer he deserved, the one he'd been waiting for.

"Well, soldier," she said, looking down at his boots, "how far are you willing to march?"

Loose Lips Sink Ships

I asked the Eskimo if he'd ever seen a vagina before.

"Because I can show you," I whispered.

Albert Huffman, a recent arrival to Fort Wayne via Alaska, was not, in fact, an Eskimo, though I would not learn this until dinner.

"Well? You wanna see it or not?" I asked, tapping my foot. I checked my watch. It was sixth grade recess. Mr. Kenning would blow the whistle any minute now. This vagina wouldn't wait around forever.

He mumbled an okay, so I motioned for him to "step into my office, soldier," and he followed me inside the bush beside the slide. The branches hid us pretty well, dousing us in half-light, and we sat on mulch chips with our legs crossed like a couple of Indians. For a moment, the whole world smelled like pine trees.

"Now, I'm not sure what you Eskimos have in the way of vagina," I began, "but here in the U.S., it looks like this." He waited, and I clapped my hands together and then split my paired hands in a V like Spock. I told him to do the same. I tilted my hands sideways and shoved my V into his V. Then, I told him to open up his palms and take a gander. He moved back some, peering in at the shadowed hole we'd created.

"Pretty sexy, huh?"

Albert waited a moment, then closed his palms.

"I guess I really don't see it."

"Whatdya mean you don't see it? Whatdya think it's supposed to look like?"

"Well, I guess I just expected . . . more," he shrugged, readjusting his shorts. "Since people are always talking about it and stuff."

"More like how, Albert?"

"I don't know . . . shinier, maybe. Or sparkly."

"Sparkly!" I laughed. "A sparkly vagina? Oh that's rich! You Eskimos are as dumb as rocks. Did you know that?" I crouched to crawl out of the bush.

"Alaska's part of the United States," he informed me, picking at a root.

"You talking to me, Eskimo?"

"You said," he explained, glancing up, "that vagina in the U.S. might look different than other vagina, like the kind in Alaska. But Alaska's part of the U.S., too."

"Well of course it is," I groaned. "Jesus H. Christ."

When Kenning blew the whistle, I told the kid to follow me. It was lunchtime, and I informed him that there wasn't any whale blubber for miles, and if he wanted to learn to eat the hot lunch and be normal like me, then he'd better stick close. I'd show him the way to the meatloaf.

"I packed my own lunch," he said, holding up a dripping brown bag. "See?"

"Yeah, I see, alright," I rolled my eyes. "But trust me, kid, that whale blubber's not gonna last forever."

And then, later that night, I discovered the difference between Eskimos and Alaskans. And also, that his dad was my dad's boss.

"You mean to tell me that an Eskimo makes a better leg than you?" I questioned.

Dad manufactures parts for handicapped people. Mostly shins and knees – pretty much anything from the thigh down. Since he works there, we got a pretty good discount on Mom's leg, "quite a perk," according to Dad.

Our Eskimo conversation took place at dinner, as Dad fumbled with his hotdog.

"Jackson, you have to understand that being the boss isn't just about who makes the best leg," he explained. "Mr. Huffman has more managerial experience. That's why they shipped him down here. And for the record, bucko," he added, "not all people from Alaska are Eskimos."

I laughed like he was joking, but then he got out the encyclopedia to prove it. I stared at a picture of a non-Eskimo Alaskan family pumping gas into a truck.

"Well, whatever your boss is," I grumbled, slamming the book, "his son's sort of a dud."

"What do you mean?" Dad asked, but I said I wasn't sure. Did he want me to say that stupid Albert didn't even know what a vagina looked like?

"Well you should be nice to him anyway," Mom said. "Since your father works with his father. Try to make him feel welcome."

"Oh, I'll make him feel welcome, all right," I chuckled, pressing the tips of my fingers together like an evil villain.

Dad pointed a fork at me.

"Hey. You better, pal."

Grinning, I pointed a fork back.

Dad and I ate Mom's cooked carrots until we felt like barfing. We didn't tell her that. We just smiled, and I said, "Mmmm," and "Now that's how you cook a carrot!" over and over again until Dad told me I was laying it on a little thick.

"Honey," Mom said to Dad midway through the meal. "You mind taking a look at the leg later? It feels a little strange."

"Strange how?"

She tapped it beneath the table. "Well, I'm not sure exactly. A little off. Hollow, almost." She was talking about her fake leg; the one God gave her after He took away the real one in a car accident back when I was just some stupid third grader.

"After dinner," he agreed, smiling, forking a carrot.

"No rush," Mom said, lumbering into the living room, collapsing on the couch. "We're not going anywhere."

From our place at the table, Dad and I could hear the T v blaring, all those cowboy bullets zinging past one another. A few more bites, then Dad put down his fork.

"All right. Better go check on that leg," he said, nodding to me like a doctor on his way to surgery. I saluted as my father moved to the living room, then peeked around the corner to watch him bend to my mother's leg, run his hands up and down the wooden shaft. From where I stood, it looked sort of stupid, like he was trying to shine a baseball bat or polish a rifle. But after awhile it started looking less stupid, like maybe he was just trying to push a little life into a dead thing.

In science class the next day, Mr. Kenning announced that we were going to learn about the wonderful world of electricity.

"Boooring," I moaned, giving it two thumbs way down.

"Jackson, would you care to explain to the class just how electricity works?" Kenning asked.

"I thought you'd never ask," I said, cracking my knuckles and scooting back my chair to stand. "You see, you flick a switch, and then the light bulbs start to buzz. Thank you for your attention."

I bowed and threw kisses to the class.

"Nope. Care to try again?"

"Magic?" I guessed, taking my seat.

"Closer," he said as he began scribbling on the chalkboard, "only there are electrons involved, and conductors."

"Listen," I said, leaning forward in my desk, beginning the speech my father taught me. "You can put glasses on a pig, but it's still gonna be a pig, only it'll look smarter."

Nobody knew quite what to say to that, not even Mr. Kenning, who turned around and adjusted his own glasses as he stared at me as if trying to solve a riddle. I leaned back in my desk, arms crossed, then winked at Albert's dumb Eskimo face.

At recess, when I asked Albert if he wanted to try again with the vagina, he said sure, that we might as well give it a shot.

"Until we get it right," I demanded, leading him back inside the bush, "because practice always makes perfect. You read me?"

We rammed our V'd hands together and took turns peering in. He peeked first, staring endlessly into a cave of darkness and mystery.

"Quit hogging, my turn," I said, then flipped our hands and investigated further, nodding. "Yup, there she is. Clear as day. Pretty as a peach."

He squinted at me.

"How do you know that's what they even look like?" Albert whispered.

"Because that's what the guys on the bus say," I explained, exasperated. "Jesus H. Christ." I slammed my hands down. "You just . . . you have to trust me on this one. You have to."

He said okay, he would.

"Really? You trust me?"

He shrugged.

"Like . . . you'd trust me with your life?"

He said maybe.

"Well, *maybe* I'll show you something else then," I said. "You're absolutely positively sure I can trust you?"

He nodded.

I eyed him.

"Because loose lips sink ships, you know that?"

"What ships?" he asked, glancing behind him. "Indiana's landlocked."

I sighed, stood up from those bushes and shrugged my shoulders. I looked to Mr. Kenning who was scanning the playground from just a few feet away.

"This one doesn't know the first thing about World War II propaganda," I explained to the teacher, pointing to the bush. "Why don't we ever learn anything useful in science, like U-boats?"

⁕ *⁕* *⁕*

Albert said his parents always came home from work kind of late, and that it was okay if he got off the bus with me, as long as my parents didn't mind. "Mind? Are you kidding?" I said. "Your dad could fire my dad. You think they're going to say no?"

For the entire bus ride home, I lectured him on Nazi Germany and American propaganda, though sometimes we took breaks to listen to what the older guys had to say about girls – all things I pretty much already knew.

"Man, I would have done three kinds of nasty with Leslie if it hadn't been for . . . well, you know," a pimply one grinned to the others.

I jumped up, swiveled my head to face them.

"You mean the period, right? The period stopped you."

They laughed, then told me that little sixth graders shouldn't be so concerned with periods. "But you're talking about Leslie, right?" I said, even though I didn't know any Leslie. I turned back around, then crouched low in the seat. I leaned over to Albert.

"See? I told you I know this stuff."

When we reached our stop, we dropped our book bags over by the rain gutter, and I told him that if he was going to help me build this fort, then he had to keep the location secret from everyone else at school.

"I don't know how things worked back in Alaska, but it's not like I would go around telling everyone about your secret igloo or whatever," I explained. "So it's the same here." He groaned, asked me to knock it off with the Eskimo stuff. I grinned at him, snapping my teeth for no reason.

"So? Where's the fort?" he asked.

I turned, wiped the smile away, then asked if he was blind.

"No."

"Well do you need glasses or something? Because maybe we can get you some glasses . . ."

There, in the woods behind my house, was a perfectly obvious pile of sticks that I'd fashioned into a fort. Maybe it wasn't much to look at just yet, but at least all the materials were there. I figured we could put something together that would be fireproof at the least, and at most, Nazi-proof.

We dragged some tools from the shed and started chopping and hacking at things. This was sort of my specialty.

"No, no, you're doing it all wrong. You got to chop like this," I explained, splitting some sticks in two with the dull axe blade. "You really have to swing it like you hate it. Show me how much you hate it, Albert."

Albert must've hated it pretty badly because by a quarter after five, we'd already split most of the sticks and managed a good foundation.

"This is the best part, though," I said, unzipping my pants and pissing into a foot-tall hollowed-out log. "Albert, meet our toilet."

Albert wanted to try, so after I finished, he peed all over the toilet log, spraying a generous coat of urine on the bark and the leaves.

"Pretty bad aim," I announced, glancing at the wet wood. "Guess you're no sharp shooter, huh, soldier?"

"My parents don't usually let me pee outdoors," he admitted.

"Oh, I get it," I said. "Because back in Alaska your wiener would probably freeze off."

He said probably.

"Tell me about it," I agreed, returning to my axe. "You're preaching to the choir on that one."

After we put the tools away and shuffled back inside, Mom introduced herself, and when Albert glanced down at her leg she joked, "My husband says it's always best to try out your own product." Albert stared at her like she was a robot, and I reminded him that it was just a leg and that it was nothing compared to what the Nazis did back in World War II.

Mom changed the subject, asking what we were doing out there in the woods. I glanced at Albert and reminded him to keep his lips tight.

"We were . . . deer hunting," I said, then corrected. "No wait, duck hunting."

Ducks seemed more likely than deer.

"Any luck?" Mom asked, reaching for the remote.

"Naw," I said, "they're all really good hiders. Deer and ducks both. Okay, well, Albert has to use the bathroom before he pees his pants again," I explained, hoping he wouldn't crack under my mother's intense questioning. "See ya!"

"Nice meeting you, Albert," she called.

In the front drive, we shot some baskets until his dad came to pick him up. He wasn't a very good shot, but I tried to be sensitive about it, figuring he probably had to shoot baskets with snowballs back in Alaska.

"Remember," I said as his father's car slowed. "Just because you're helping me build the fort doesn't mean you can go blabbing about it."

He said he knew, that I didn't have to remind him every five seconds.

"Well I'm counting on you, soldier," I said, giving him a salute. He waved, and as his dad rolled down the window I said, "Hey mister, my mom thinks you make a pretty great leg." Then I waved and smiled until my face nearly split.

I wondered if they made fake faces, too.

✳ ✳ ✳

That night, after Mom and Dad interrogated me further about what we were doing in the woods, I grabbed some blank paper and watercolors and painted a picture entitled "Mesopotamia." Basically, it was just a lot of brown huts next to one another and a purple dragon flying overhead.

"Why 'Mesopotamia'?" Albert asked the following day when I showed him my masterpiece.

"You don't know the first thing about Mesopotamia, do you?" I asked. "Jesus!"

He shrugged and then walked off.

It was recess again, but we didn't make vaginas. Instead, he played soccer with some of the other guys, while a pack of loud, snarling girls clapped and cheered and told them that they had good ball control.

Jessica Meyers, the most annoying of all, could whistle really loud by slipping two fat fingers into her mouth and kind of jerking her neck like she was choking. She was the girl who always raised her hand in class to point out something like, "Um . . . Mr. Kenning, did you know that ninety percent of the world is covered with water?" to which he would reply, "No, stupid, it's actually closer to seventy percent."

I'm paraphrasing.

Probably, I would have given in and played soccer, too, if it wasn't for "Mesopotamia." But I wanted to keep it safe, and there was no way I could trust one of those spectator girls to keep an eye on it while I scored all the goals. Probably, their hand sweat would ruin the paper and smear the dragon, too.

So I rolled it up and wandered up and down the sidewalk, watching as some ants crawled back and forth from the grass to a little dirt mound by the baseball field. I wondered what they looked like under a magnifying glass, but I didn't want to risk it in case I fried them, and also, I'd left mine at home.

After a few minutes of ant observation, I went back to watching the soccer game because I didn't really care about those stupid ants anyway. Instead, I cared about how those idiot boys stumbled over the ball and rolled their ankles and limped around like they'd just taken a bullet from a Nazi storm trooper. I made it my policy never to play with boys like that – the kind who didn't know anything. They made for the worst soldiers.

Albert was bigger than the others, and after he scored a goal – after all those dumb girls stood up and cheered for him like he was the coolest thing since alternating current – I stood to leave, waving goodbye to my ant friends, leaving them to crawl and die in Albert's dust.

✳ ✳ ✳

Mom's leg did not grow back. This was a misconception I had about the healing process back when I was some moron kid. For some reason, I was under the impression that maybe legs could grow back the way skin did. Just give it enough time to scab over and sure enough, inch by inch . . .

Dad straightened me out pretty quickly. I remember him crying while Mom was still in the hospital, and when I told him not to worry, that surely it'd grow back, he kissed me and said it was a beautiful thought, but it was wrong to believe in miracles.

"But it's called Miracle-Gro for crying out loud!"

He said that was just for plants.

I never did understand the prosthetic completely. She didn't sleep with it, and some nights, I'd peer in their darkened bedroom just to see its shadow loom against the wall like a sentinel.

Once, on TBS, they were playing *The Christmas Story*, and when they showed that leg lamp, I turned to Mom, tapped her own leg, and said, "Hey, probably, it'd make for a pretty good lamp, huh?" She and Dad both thought this very cute at the time. Only it became less cute when, on Christmas morning, I put a shade over the top and placed it in the living room under the tree. Dad had to carry Mom in just to see it. Turned out I was the only one laughing.

When Albert and I returned to our fort a few days later, I told him he was kind of like a prosthetic himself.

"You know, like you're good to have around," I admitted, "but it's not like I'd die without you."

"Okaaaaaaaay," he said, drawing the word out for an entire breath. "I get it."

I looked over, then told him he'd have to stack the wood tighter, that if we wanted to stretch ripped trash bags over the top for a roof, then we'd need to get serious with the walls. And we needed to get serious to keep the rainwater out, too, which was a necessity since I'd decided to display "Mesopotamia" in the fort. I'd placed it in a temporary safe spot beside the toilet log.

"So what's with you playing soccer lately?" I asked, my tongue dangling from my mouth as I returned to digging the booby trap hole just beyond the entrance. "I thought you and me could hang out in that bush some more. Keep practicing until you get it right."

He restacked the sticks and pressed them tight like I told him, then wound some old kite string around them to hold everything steady.

"Soccer's more fun," he explained. "Especially scoring goals. No offense, but all that vagina stuff was getting kind of weird and boring."

What would the guys in the back of the bus think if I told them that? If I said, "Hey guys, this Eskimo over here thinks vaginas are weird and boring." Probably, we'd all have a good laugh, and then maybe we'd shove Albert's head into his crotch until he admitted he'd made a terrible mistake, that they were the farthest thing from weird or boring, more like normal and exciting.

The woods were quiet then, and peaceful, and I dug that hole until it was about three feet deep, and then I picked some thorns. I filled the hole with a layer of thorns, and I covered it with leaves. I'd pricked myself a few times, sure, but it felt good to know exactly what trespassers had coming to them.

"Now don't forget to step to the side," I warned, dabbing a foot gently on the leaf-covered trap. "And don't go telling anyone about this or else it's useless. Loose lips sink . . ."

"Shit!" Albert cried.

"Um . . . no, it's actually ships," I explained, "with a -p."

Then I looked a bit closer to notice that he'd gotten his finger stuck between some logs, so I figured maybe he'd meant what he said.

Since he was from Alaska, I doubted Albert was the crying type. Probably, he'd killed polar bears after school when nothing good was on television. So when I saw him curled up on the forest floor rocking like a baby, I put the shovel down and leaned over him, expecting the worst – a severed hand.

"I'm a doctor, let me see," I ordered, shoving one hand away from the other. I knelt on the ground beside him, my knees in the dirt, and I spread his fingers apart to examine each one individually. I held my grip on the ring finger.

"It's this one, isn't it?" I guessed, touching the crooked, bloated one. He nodded, winced, peered out over the tree limbs to avoid looking at it. "Yup, just as I suspected," I sighed.

I extended the finger and a humming sound came from his throat, kind of like the water heater in the hallway closet.

"Okay, let me grab the shovel," I offered, wiping the dirt from my palms. "I think we can cut it off and still save the hand."

"No," he cried. "I'm fine, really."

But I was already back on my feet, walking toward the shovel.

"Hey, don't worry about it," I assured him, reaching for the wooden handle. "One of our dads can get you a real good deal on a new one."

✳   ✳   ✳

Turned out, a Band-Aid was sufficient. And some rubbing alcohol. And a squirt of Cortizone-10.

"See? I told you we could save the hand."

He thanked me and said I was a pretty good guy, especially since I hadn't chopped off his hand.

"Well I wanted to," I began, "and I would have if it came to that."

He nodded.

"Hey," I said, pausing, "does this mean we can be friends at school tomorrow?"

He said okay, if that's what I wanted.

It was, so I locked his hand in a tight grip to solidify our friendship, but that only made him scream all over again.

Long story short, we were friends again. Allies. And for the whole next day, we walked around the playground together, and I showed him my ant friends, and he dabbed at them with his swollen finger

"Sometimes I like to . . . kill 'em," I lied, then surprise attacked a herd of them and just mashed down hard with my shoe. I wanted to show him I was serious, and that I'd do pretty much anything to make sure people feared me.

"Geez, man," he said, pulling his finger back, "you didn't have to kill them."

"It was nothing," I assured, wiping my shoe on the grass. "I swear."

Then stupid Jessica and some of her friends came over, and they all said hi. Every single one of them said hi. Like ten different people all saying hi. Like a machine gun.

"Hi, hi, hi, hi, hi," I said, and Albert offered a small wave.

"Uh . . . can we help you with something?" I asked in a deep voice, flexing like a weightlifter. Jessica turned to Albert and handed him a note. Then, in a spray of ponytails the girls were gone, and I ran after them, clicking my tongue like how cowboys do to cattle.

"Man, you never have a crossbow when you need one," I sighed, then turned to Albert. "Sorry about them."

He uncrumpled the note.

"What is it?" I asked. "She want to be your girlfriend or something?"

He said yes, that's what it was.

"Well, trust me," I explained, V-ing my hands. "A guy like you can do better."

❋   ❋   ❋

That night, Mom and I were watching television when I realized I'd forgotten all about "Mesopotamia." I'd left it in the woods the day Albert nearly lost his finger.

Had it rained recently? Was it ruined?

There are a lot of things about that painting that other people probably wouldn't understand. Like why I drew a purple dragon over the city. It's simple, really: because even though there were no purple dragons there, there were great warriors, so I figured why not give them a dragon to deal with? People usually think I'm pretty dumb until I stop and explain things to them. Then, they usually think I'm pretty smart. And also, people never know a masterpiece when they see one – I overheard Dad say this once as he stroked Mom's leg in the dark.

I stood up, slipped my shoes on, then hummed a patriotic song I didn't know the words to and began marching valiantly toward the woods.

Already, it was late fall and the leaves formed a nice cushion on the ground. Probably, I didn't have to wear shoes at all. Everything was brown and burned-smelling and crackled as I walked.

There, in the woods, I saw the last person I expected to see. Actually, I hadn't expected to see anyone because the booby trap hadn't been tripped, but there she was, dumb as ever, Jessica Meyers. She was just leaning against the wall we'd constructed from sticks.

I froze like a polar bear.

Where were our weapons? Where were our goddamn weapons?

I hid behind a few trees, watching the top half of her body squirm as she peered down at the ground, eyes wide and mouth open. I couldn't see the rest of her – just that floating t-shirt – and then, a moment later there was Albert, rising like a prince, growing from the ground.

Something suspiciously sexual was going on; I could sense it.

"A-ha!" I said, revealing myself. "You!"

Jessica bent down, tugged up her shorts, then returned to standing.

"Why the heck are her pants down?" I cried to Albert. "Someone could get rabies for crying out loud!"

"Jackson?" Albert whispered. He was scared of me. Real scared. I stomped my feet the way Dad did when the raccoons knocked over the trash cans.

"Git! Git outta here! Scat! Move on!"

"Jackson, hold up . . ."

"You're . . . you're putting glasses on a pig, Albert!" I stuttered, pointing to her. Jessica covered her face with her hands.

"Let's see those glasses, pig," I said, clawing at her arms. "Go ahead, show 'em off, piggie!"

She ran behind Albert like he'd protect her – her heroic, fake Eskimo.

"And you," I said, pointing a finger at him like a curse. Snot ran down my face, and I tried to suck it in. "Mr. . . . Mr. 'I-think-va-ginas-are-weird-and-boring.' If they're so weird and boring, then what were you two doing back here? Making some kind of weird and boring hot sex?"

I stamped again, snapping, growling – like maybe I was the one with the rabies.

I waited for him to explain everything and make us friends again, but he didn't.

My chest throbbed, and I really wanted to kick things and break things and throw spears.

Where *were* all the goddamn spears?

I buckled, caught myself against a tree branch.

"Well?" I asked at last.

"Well what?"

"You tell me, soldier!"

"We were just . . ." Jessica began.

I stuffed my fingers in my ears and began humming until she shut her big, fat pig lips and ran out of the woods. Her butt looked as big as the moon. Bigger even.

Then, it was just me and the Eskimo all over again.

"Well?" I repeated. "What do you have to say for yourself?"

"I don't know, Jackson," he shrugged. "I guess . . . this is what we're supposed to be doing now."

I rolled my eyes until I could practically see my brain.

"Says who? Supreme Allied Commander Dwight D. Eisenhower?"

He didn't answer.

Far off, the rumble of a car going elsewhere. The sound of my sniffling.

Maybe, I considered as we stood there, we could just wait here forever. Until we grew beards and got arthritis and all our limbs peeled away. Maybe this fort could be like our new home, and those ants from school – the ones that survived, anyhow – they could move in with us. Maybe the dragon from "Mesopotamia" could even pull guard duty to make sure no idiotic girls or Nazis ever tried to breach our barrier.

I wanted to tell him all of these things, about how good we could have it if we wanted.

Instead, I just whispered, "Albert, I think you have the loosest lips of anyone."

He nodded, said he understood, that he wouldn't return to our fort any longer.

I saluted him with one hand and gave him the middle finger with the other. I figured I owed him that much.

He turned to leave but stopped. I thought maybe the idiot's shoestring had come untied but it hadn't. Not by a long shot.

"Go away," I ordered. "That is, unless you want a spear in your heart."

Still, he just moved closer.

"So what? Are you going to murder me like some common polar bear?" I asked.

He shook his head no, offered me the V of his hands, waited for me to enter.

Robotics

I made this robot. Everyone was making them. Mine was a vacuum cleaner with a rubber jack-o-lantern mask taped to the handle. His name was Z-Bot2131F, but I just called him Brady, after my dead brother. Brady, my brother, had come out cold, and then we buried him in Lindenwood Cemetery, and then, directly following, we cried. Just a few weeks later, we started going to church more and more. Then, I taped the mask to the handle.

Everyone in the neighborhood thought Brady was pretty great, and sometimes I'd wheel him around the sidewalks, and kids like Joseph Ames and Ryan Curl would come trickling from their houses to ask questions about how he worked and how I'd built him.

"Does he understand English?" Ryan asked, and I said, "Oh yeah, and a little Spanish, too."

"Well, what does he do?" asked Joseph, and I said, "Two things. Watch."

I wheeled my robot inside Joseph's house, and I plugged him into the wall. Then, I pretended to check invisible dials and cranks. I made some beeping sounds with my mouth and acted nervous, like he might explode or something if he wasn't properly handled. "Get back!" I cried, and I stood back myself to add to the suspense.

Joseph's cat – a tabby named Mushu began brushing up against the side of my robot, and that's when I pressed down hard on the switch. Brady burst to life – something my brother had never done – and as the light flashed on the front panel, Mushu took off up the stairs, hissing. I grinned, guided Brady along the floor some, and we all listened to the chortle and cough of that robot hard at work. That jack-o'-lantern mask was always loose. It fell off sometimes when the tape got warm or damp or collected too many Mushu hairs. After a few minutes of my demonstration, I killed the switch, and I ran my hand over the top of the handle.

"Yup. So far I've trained him to do two things," I reviewed. "He scares cats and he vacuums carpets." Neither of them thought this impressive, so I told them that he could scare dogs, too, at least small, cowardly ones. They shrugged and began talking basketball.

"Well how about this," I tried, waving my arms to get their attention. "I'll let you guys spend the night and we'll order pizzas, and I'll help you build robots like mine." This, they agreed, sounded pretty good, especially the pizza, and I said great, then it was settled.

When Brady and I stepped inside the house, Mom rose from the table, asking where I had been, and why I had the vacuum, and how dare I vanish without telling her.

"Mom," I said. "Who vanished? We just went for a walk."

"And it didn't cross your mind to inform me?" I shook my head no. It hadn't. I slapped the top of the vacuum like maybe it could be his fault instead. She closed her eyes and rubbed her temples and said, "Come on, Dylan, you have to try harder for me now, okay?" I said okay. "Because the last thing I need is for you to disappear like that." I nodded. She opened her eyes and winced at the lights.

147

"Maybe you and Z-bot should go to your room for awhile and think about things."

I said fine, even though I didn't know what "things" I was supposed to be thinking about.

"But you have to order pizza," I called before closing the door. "Cuz Ryan and Joe are spending the night tonight." Mom laughed, said no they weren't, not in this house. When I asked why not, she slipped the workout tape into the mouth of the VCR and spread her mat on the floor.

"It's a school night, remember?"

I groaned, but I didn't get angry.

We could blame Mom for a lot of things, but we couldn't blame her for Thursday.

❋   ❋   ❋

Snug between sheets, Brady and I slept together, alongside a few stuffed animals – tigers and bears and a dolphin. The vacuum was cold, so I buried it in plush, and if I tried hard enough, I almost couldn't feel a thing.

Some nights, when I couldn't sleep, I made up dreams. I pretended to sleep and then I pretended to wake, and then I pretended to see that vacuum come alive. Sometimes Brady's human voice would come from the inside of the vacuum bag. It would say things like, "Help! It's me! It's your baby brother! I've been right here all along!" Sometimes, there wouldn't be any sounds at all, just a punching from inside, a tiny fist jabbing for the zipper. I didn't want to make a big deal out of it, but I mentioned it to Mom, that Brady, the baby, had been waking me up at night.

"Waking you up how?"

"I don't know. Scratching from the inside of the vacuum bag and stuff."

Mom grabbed my hand and dragged me to tell my father.

"It's official. You're crazy," Dad said to Mom, then glanced at me. "And you, too. You're crazy for making her crazy." I returned to my room while they continued to talk.

"Can't we all just move on already?" he called a few minutes later, but since I'd just plugged Brady in, I pretended not to hear a thing.

✻ ✻ ✻

One night, Ryan Curl came over and set to work building a robot from a skateboard and a broken telephone. Meanwhile, I made a few modifications to Brady. First, I slipped one of baby Brady's miniature shirts around the vacuum handle and straightened it to match up with the mask. Next, I unknotted the cord, then set to work polishing the wheels with a rag and water.

Ryan's robot was pretty bad – it was certainly no Brady – and when he caught me staring at the curling wires on the skateboard deck, he said, "It may not look like much, but it can think like a human."

"Think like a human how?"

"Watch," he said, tapping a few numbers on the remainder of the phone base before shoving the skateboard across the living room with his foot.

"I programmed him to do that," he explained, proud. I rolled my eyes and told him mine could think like a human, too, and to prove it, plugged Brady in and listened to him whir.

Mom walked into the room to tell us to knock it off, but then she glimpsed baby Brady's shirt on robot Brady's body, and she didn't yell one bit. She wore sweatpants because she was always wearing sweatpants then, and then she turned him off, pointed to Brady, whispered, "Dylan, how could you?"

"But . . . Brady said to," I whimpered. "In a dream." Mom slammed the vacuum to the floor before tripping over Ryan's robot and scattering the numbered keys. Ryan watched everything from his place on the floor, and when Mom left, I leaned over to him, cupped my hand to his ear:

"My robot makes people cry. Can yours?"

Missing Mary

You've heard this one before.

A sophomore at the local high school struggles through the periodic table.

The symbols aren't the problem. She understands that B is for boron and C is for carbon, she even knows the trickier ones. What she doesn't know are their atomic weights or how to find them, what the teacher means when he says valence. On her teacher's recommendation, she seeks out a tutor who we'll call Tim, though that's not his real name, but it's good enough and you get the picture. And we'll call her Mary because this, too, will help put a face on things.

After Tuesday's final bell, Mary catches Tim beside his locker, introduces herself, and he stares at her for a while before saying something like, "Yeah, I know who you are."

Mary smiles, which is what she always does when she wants things.

"Valence," she admits. "And atomic weights."

He nods and picks at his nails, but he's a teenager – don't read too much into this.

"So?" she tries. "Can you help?"

Tim – who's maybe a little strange but no more so than any other tenth grader – agrees he probably can.

"Meet me at the library at 8:00?" he asks.

He'll be at a table near the back.

Fast-forward a few hours, and Tim has just finished pork chops with his family. His father reads the paper while he chews, but this won't prove a critical detail. Tim excuses himself upstairs to wet his hair. This, too, won't prove critical. Nor will what the family dog is doing (rummaging through the neighbor's trash).

It's never quite clear what Mary is doing during this time, as Tim finishes his dinner, as the dog gnaws on a corncob next door. She had soccer practice until 5:30 – we know this much – but there are discrepancies after that. Most teammates swear she waved goodbye and started home, though one refutes the claim.

She was going to see her boyfriend. You know she had a boyfriend, right?

Meanwhile, Mary's mother and father are watching their youngest daughter's dress rehearsal for *The Wind in the Willows* (Mary's sister plays Stoat #2), and while her mother left a note – *Leftovers in the fridge, sweetie* – it's unclear if Mary ever entered the house to read it.

The library closes at 9:00, and at 8:15, when she still has not arrived, Tim begins wondering why he asked her to meet him so late. An hour, let alone forty-five minutes, was hardly enough time to cover anything. The alkalines if they were lucky, though they wouldn't stand a chance with noble gases.

He sits at the back table and examines his notes, though the truth is, he rarely needs them. Chemistry has always come naturally to Tim, though it's mostly a thankless gift.

It is a fine library with an excess of hardcover books, subscriptions to major newspapers, enough microfilm to blanket the town in its past.

Though perhaps this doesn't matter.

What matters is that Tim waits for her until the librarian begins tapping the face of her watch. She doesn't have to clear her throat.

He nods, gathers his things, slips past the empty chair beside him.

❊   ❊   ❊

You know how things go from here.

Her parents call the police, the obligatory squad car arrives, and a pair of bulging-bellied officers extricate themselves from the bucket seats of their cruiser and flip open their pocket-sized pads. Except maybe one of them isn't all that fat. Maybe the other makes up for his fatness.

"Okeedokee, so when was the last time you saw the little lady?"

"You recall how she was dressed?"

"And how might you describe her mental state?"

Mary's mother fumbles through all of these while Mary's father feigns distraction with the thermostat, turning the wheel and watching the needle follow. He sets it at a comfortable seventy-four, appreciating this power between his fingers.

Mary's little sister – who performed admirably as Stoat #2 throughout her dress rehearsal – is unsure how to interpret all these strangers in her house. She hides in the kitchen with chocolate milk, rehearsing her line in her head.

Half an hour later, when Mary's father discovers Mary's little sister there, he plops her atop his knee, assuring her that everything will be just fine.

Mary is most likely just out with friends, he explains, reciting his own line. *The obvious answer is most often the right one.*

And then it's morning. Mary's mother has not slept and her father has managed only an hour or two. No one attempts breakfast, though what concerns Mary's sister is that she's given permission to stay home from school.

She thinks:

Somebody must be sick.

She thinks:

But there is no understudy for Stoat #2!

The officers have multiplied. They are in every stairwell and closet, each of them gripping a Styrofoam cup in one hand and a bear claw in the other. One of the officers offers a bear claw to the father. He declines.

"You know, we get these calls all the time," an officer says between bites. "Nine times out of ten they're just out blowing off steam."

Mary's father nods because it is easy and his head remembers how.

He wonders:

What kind of steam?

* * *

Two policemen walk into a high school.

The first one says, "We'll need to have a look inside her locker."

And the second one says, "Yes, indeedy we will."

Inside it: books, a dried flower, a mirror.

One officer gets it in his head to examine the flower, as if implicating it. It's a purple flower, its petals brittle, though the officer is uncertain in placing its time of death.

And then, a breakthrough:

"You know, she *was* having trouble with valence," admits Mary's science teacher upon questioning. "I think his name was..."

They pull Tim from Spanish class in the middle of conjugating *jugar.*

"Heard you and the girl were study partners?"

"No," he tells them. "We were supposed to meet at the library but didn't."

No, he wouldn't consider them close friends.

No, he hardly knew her.

"Then why did she approach you?" they ask. "You of all people."

He shrugs, reminds them it's not a crime to be good at chemistry.

"You two fool around, Timmy?" an officer asks.

He says no; that was the chemistry he wasn't good at.

They can't find a body. They refuse to call it murder.

Sometimes people just . . . disappear.

Some nights Mary's mother imagines Mary living beneath an oak tree in a faraway woods. She imagines baskets overflowing with ripened blackberries and glass bottles of milk kept cool in the streams. It is not a leisurely life she imagines, but it is a good life, and in it, her daughter is always well fed.

Mary's father's faith is different.

"It'll be easier the sooner we come to terms with it. We just need to try to bear it."

There's an inquest, witnesses lining up in their finest attire as if it's picture day. There is a surplus of boys, many of which describe themselves as former boyfriends or former acquaintances or "just some guy from a party."

Every last one of them touched her, Mary's father thinks, *or at least they know who did.*

The only one he doesn't blame is the pale boy from Mary's school. He can't remember all the names, but the shaky one, the pale-faced chemistry kid. The boy is a ghost or almost, his eyelids drooping, and Mary's father can't imagine him being capable of much of anything, let alone making his daughter disappear.

"And the last time you saw her was beside your locker, is that correct?" a suited man asks, tapping a fifty dollar pen against a table.

"Yes, sir."

"And she didn't show up at the library as planned?"

"No, sir," he agrees. "She did not."

Tim is free to go. They thank him for his time.

"Sir," Tim says, standing, and the suited man turns.

"I don't know if it's important or not, but . . . she needed help with the periodic table."

"Is that so?"

Tim nods dutifully.

"I don't know if it's important," he repeats, "but I wanted to tell someone. In case it means something."

In a scratchpad, Mary's father writes: Periodic table.

The suited man thanks him, and Mary's father peeks up from his pad to watch the pale boy mouth, "You're welcome."

❋   ❋   ❋

The mystery rattles the town until it doesn't. One day, the newspapers just find better things to write.

There is a problem with the city's waste management. Later, a corruption of the city comptroller.

The police chief tells Mary's family that the investigation "has run its course" and the clues are "few and far between."

"But let's never lose hope," he says, clutching Mary's mother's hand the way he's clutched dozens before. "Things just have a way of . . . showing up."

But she is not a lost sock, Mary's mother thinks. She is not a set of keys.

Mary's name is forgotten (though, remember, that's not even her real name), and since there is no indication that she is dead, the newspaper refuses to run an obituary – sparing itself the correction if she is found living.

Nor does the school hold a memorial in her honor.

After holiday break the principal clutches the microphone in his office and announces that grief counselors are available to students. He isn't implying anything, he informs them, it's just an announcement.

❋   ❋   ❋

It's spring, and a fisherman whose name isn't important stops his motorboat at the edge of a shore. A burlap sack half buoyed in the water. He almost continues on, but stops.

Please refrain from speculation.

For whatever reason he kills the engine. Leans over the boat and pulls it toward him. Everything shifts.

Probably a deer out of season, avoiding a fine.

❋   ❋   ❋

It is not her, not a deer, just garbage.

She is not in the sack, and she is not in the quarry. Six months later, she is not in the Dumpster, either. She is not in the chemistry lab or the library, nor is she (or her sister) backstage at the elementary school.

A few years come and go like principals.

There are no sightings – not even glimpses – and everyone who remembers Mary soon forgets.

Her friends, her teammates.

Even Tim. And that's all there is to say about him.

The police chief notes what appear to be bone fragments from the insides of burlap sacks and quarries. They are never Mary's.

Over a Thanksgiving break, one group assembles in somebody's basement where they sip a few beers, snack on stale chips.

Around midnight, somebody says, "Hey, remember that one girl?" and someone else says, "Who?"

They are talking about the girl who got pregnant their senior year.

Nobody anywhere is talking about Mary.

Eventually, even Mary's parents forget – as much as parents can – which is to say they don't forget at all. They cannot even forget the way she once tucked herself tightly inside a sleeping bag. And how each movie stub she ever saved marked a time and a date from her past. To Mary's parents, everything in the world seems to be rubbing it in: a hairbrush, a nail file, a music box, a bra, the ant farm in the back of her closet. Worst of all, in Mary's sock drawer sits the skeletal remains of a bouquet caught at her cousin's wedding – another prophecy unfulfilled.

Meanwhile, Mary's younger sister searches for her in the crawl space and the attic and the closet beneath the stairs. Once, upon discovering a pair of pink earmuffs, she begins to understand that her missing sister is everywhere and nowhere all at once. Yes, of course, she is the stain on the hallway carpet and the half-full bottle of perfume, but also she is neither of these things. *A memory,* Mary's sister decides, *is only a memory for as long as you care to remember.*

Years later, as Mary's sister sits silently in chemistry class, science will give her an answer:

My sister has simply turned soluble.

A moment there and then gone.

Credits

"The Clowns," previously published in *Flying House*, 2010

"Dixie Land," previously published in *The Barcelona Review*, 2009

"Indian Village," previously published in
    Berkeley Fiction Review, 2011

"Line of Scrimmage," previously published
    in *Annalemma Magazine*, 2009

"Loose Lips Sink Ships," previously published
    in *Mid-American Review*, 2008

"Missing Mary," previously published in *American
    Short Fiction*, web exclusive, 2010

"Robotics," previously published in the *Bellingham Review*, 2008

"Schooners," previously published in *Faultline*, 2010

"Sightings," previously published in *The Southeast Review*, 2010

"Westward Expansion," previously published in *Barrelhouse*,
    2010

B. J. HOLLARS is author of *Thirteen Loops: Race, Violence and the Last Lynching in America* (2011) and *Opening the Doors: The Desegregation of the University of Alabama and the Fight for Civil Rights in Tuscaloosa* (2013). He is editor of *You Must Be This Tall to Ride: Contemporary Writers Take You Inside the Story* (2009), *Monsters: A Collection of Literary Sightings* (2012), and *Blurring the Boundaries: Explorations to the Fringes of Nonfiction* (2013). He lives in Wisconsin with his family, where he is an assistant professor of creative writing at the University of Wisconsin-Eau Claire.

CPSIA information can be obtained at www.ICGtesting.com
Printed in the USA
LVOW130433280213

322023LV00003B/5/P